"A little more, baby," Betina said as she urged Maxine to lean back as far as possible. "That's it."

Maxine loved the way Betina touched her when time and space were at a premium. They knew how to please each other in almost any situation or location, and could get right to the point at a moment's notice. A fleeting thought flashed in Maxine's head as she imagined sharing this story with her best friend, Elaine Marcaluso, at breakfast. *She'll never believe Betina had her hand in my pants on a carnival ride*, she thought with a chuckle.

Visit

Bella Books

at

BellaBooks.com

or call our toll-free number

1-800-729-4992

White Lace
and
Promises

PEGGY J. HERRING

Bella
BOOKS
2004

Bella Books, Inc.
P.O. Box 10543
Tallahassee, FL 32302

Printed in the United States of America on acid-free paper
First Edition

Editor: Anna Chinappi
Cover designer: Sandy Knowles

ISBN 1-931513-73-2

For Stormy

Acknowledgments

I would like to thank Frankie J. Jones, always my first reader. I depend on your impressions and I value your opinion. You've never failed to help me write a better book.

I want to thank Linda Hill for her support and encouragement. You're doing a great job and I appreciate all of your hard work.

Thanks also go to Pat Gilliatt from Hairmax of Roswell. I never knew how truly complicated hair could be.

I would like to thank Dr. L. Renee Boyd for answering my never ending list of medical questions. Your attention to detail was refreshing and your enthusiasm is always a delight.

I want to also thank Martha Cabrera for the brainstorming sessions over fried chicken. I look forward to having many more of those!

A special thanks to Laverne Bell for being my second reader. You helped make this a stronger novel. You are an inspiration and a blessing in my life.

About the Author

Peggy J. Herring lives on seven acres of mesquite in south Texas with her cockatiel, hermit crabs and two wooden cats. When she isn't writing, Peggy enjoys fishing and traveling. She is the author of *Love's Harvest, Hot Check, Those Who Wait* from Naiad Press and *White Lace and Promises, Calm Before the Storm, The Comfort of Strangers* and *Beyond All Reason* from Bella Books. In addition, Peggy has contributed short stories to several Naiad anthologies, including *The First Time Ever, Dancing In the Dark, Lady Be Good, The Touch of Your Hand,* and *The Very Thought of You.* Peggy is currently working on a new romance titled *Midnight Rain* to be released by Bella Books in 2005.

Once More With Feeling and *To Have and To Hold,* originally published by Naiad Press, will also be available from Bella Books in 2004.

Chapter One

Maxine saw the chaos up ahead and slowed down. Cars on both sides of the interstate were stopping and a few people began leaving their vehicles, running toward the accident. Maxine scrambled out of her car as well and hurried to help a teenage girl and a cowboy get an older man from a wrecked, smoking pickup. The teenager, thin, blond and looking like a thousand other young girls her age, had been a passenger in the truck, but seemed to be moving around just fine. The man who had been driving, however, wasn't as lucky. The smell of gasoline spurred everyone to get the injured out of the vehicles and as far away from the accident as possible.

"Put him over here," Maxine said, and moved out of the way while a swarm of good Samaritans carried the man to a grassy area on the side of the road. Giving the teenager another quick visual inspection, Maxine asked if she was hurt anywhere.

"Not really. I had my seat belt on."

"You a nurse or somethin'?" came a deep male voice beside them. It was the cowboy.

"Not exactly," Maxine replied, making it a point not to mention that she was a doctor. She had no desire to be held responsible for anything that happened here, whether it be good or bad. Lawsuits for malpractice under any circumstances were almost automatic these days, but Maxine chose not to think about that at the moment. To not render aid when it was needed was unthinkable; however, she did find it a point of contention that for a woman to know anything about medicine, she would have to be a nurse instead of a doctor. It had been a pet peeve of hers since medical school, but she had mellowed over the years and had long since stopped being vocal about it. She raised an eyelid on the unconscious man as blood oozed from a gash on his head.

"Thanks for stopping anyway," the cowboy said as he knelt down beside her. "You act like you know what you're doin'. I wasn't looking forward to starting that artificial 'semination stuff on this guy."

At a glance, Maxine took in the cowboy's new starched Wrangler jeans, a turquoise western shirt, a black cowboy hat, and shiny black boots. His belt buckle was the size of a hubcap and caught the sun just right, temporarily blinding everyone around him. He had a kind face and didn't seem to mind getting blood on his outfit, so Maxine welcomed his help.

"It's resuscitation," she said as she checked the victim's pulse. "It's artificial resuscitation, not insemination. Can you see if someone has called 911? And check on anyone else who might need help in the other cars."

"Is he dead?" the teenager asked. Her eyes were wide and her young face had drained of all color. "Is my dad gonna die?"

"He's got a nasty bump on his head," Maxine said.

The man moaned and reached a hand out for his daughter. She grabbed it and held on tightly. The heat from the truck, which was now fully engulfed in flames, made the accident seem a lot closer than it actually was, and frightening in its intensity. People shouted warnings all around them and cars honked up and down the highway while impatient drivers sat parked in traffic. The wail of a siren could be heard in the distance and made Maxine feel better. A fire truck finally pulled up and added new chaos to the scene.

"More help's on the way," Maxine said to the teenager. Taking off her windbreaker, Maxine used the soft lining of a sleeve to get some of the blood out of the man's eyes. The laceration on his head would require several stitches, but the blood flow was easing and he was breathing on his own. Hopefully, things looked much worse than they actually were.

"There's a lady in the other car that ain't doin' so good," the cowboy said as he squatted down beside them and nodded toward a badly crumpled Ford Escort.

"Okay. Thanks," Maxine said. She smiled reassuringly at the young girl and gave her shoulder a squeeze. "Talk to him. Keep him awake."

Maxine jogged over to the other car to see if there was anything she could do for its occupants. A police officer had arrived and a few minutes later the firemen had the pickup's fire contained. By the time emergency medical services roared to a stop, Maxine had both injured people in the Escort as stable as she could get them under the circumstances. Once EMS arrived, Maxine's medical obligations were over. The paramedics were in charge.

"Well, look at you!" Junior Stevens said as he flashed Maxine his toothy grin. He jumped out of the ambulance and let his partner get their equipment from the back. "What have we got here, Doc? Did you have to put 'em all in stirrups before you could examine any-body?" Knowing Dr. Maxine Weston as a popular obstetrician and gynecologist, Junior Stevens snickered at his own silly joke.

"Cute, Junior. Don't forget how much your wife likes visiting me in my office."

He laughed and then they both became serious again. Maxine pointed toward the mangled Escort. "A broken clavicle on the pas-senger and a bruised chest on the driver from the airbag. A concussion for the male on the ground over there. He and his daughter were in the pickup. All yours now. Good luck."

Okay, she thought. *I've turned the trauma victims over to the authorities, but I'd better stay around in case they need me.*

Junior nodded and smiled. "Hey, Doc," he said before lowering his voice and leaning toward her to whisper, "you give me a call the next time you and your girlfriend want another little ride in my ambulance." He winked and she could tell by his expression that he was sincere. Maxine smiled and had a feeling she was blushing.

She stayed and helped until all the injured were transported and traffic was finally beginning to move around the scene of the accident again. Tow trucks maneuvered through flares and broken glass to get the vehicles out of the way. A while later she found her windbreaker neatly folded on the grass. The blood on the sleeve had dried already. She tossed it over her shoulder with every intention of throwing it in the washer once she got home.

"Looks like everybody's gonna make it," the cowboy said when he reached his truck. He had bloodstains all over his new shirt. "You done good, ma'am."

"Thanks," Maxine said. "So did you." She opened her car door as traffic continued to crawl past them.

"Hey," he called. "What's your name? I've got a clean shirt in my truck here. Let's get somethin' to eat somewhere and pat each other on the back."

"I can't. Sorry."

The cowboy touched the brim of his hat and grinned. "Artificial resuscitation," he said, careful to pronounce each word correctly. "Not insemination. I got confused in all the excitement earlier and said the wrong thing."

Maxine chuckled. "So maybe the guy didn't have a concussion after all. Maybe he just passed out once he heard what you had in mind for him."

The cowboy shrugged and laughed. "Yeah, maybe."

❧

4

"As long as you were out there saving lives, I guess it's okay that you're late," Betina said in that teasing tone she had sometimes.

Maxine watched her lover walk around their bedroom with nothing on but black spiked heels and black bikini underwear. Betina's breasts were large and firm, and Maxine could easily imagine herself spending the rest of her life propped up in bed watching Betina rummage through closets and dresser drawers looking for the right thing to wear. It literally took Betina hours to get dressed sometimes, and Maxine would bet money that Betina had been wearing exactly what she had on for a good part of the afternoon.

"Did you check your desk calendar at the office today?" Betina asked sweetly.

Maxine laughed. Betina had been in Maxine's office earlier in the week and had written reminders about Valentine's Day on her calendar. Maxine stuck her foot out when Betina passed close by the bed.

"I'll remember. I'll remember," Maxine said. "I've got something interesting already planned for us."

"Is Woody covering for you?" Betina asked as she let Maxine's foot slowly work its way up her thigh. "I don't want you getting paged while we're out doing whatever it is you've got planned."

"I've taken care of it already." Their eyes met and Maxine could see that little twinkling look Betina always got when she was aroused. "But it means I'm covering for him on Easter, so no fair giving me a hard time when the Easter Bunny doesn't bring you new toys in a timely manner this year, okay?"

Betina eased Maxine back on the bed and straddled her body. "Then I'll just have to leave little bunny-notes on your calendar a lot earlier than usual, now won't I?"

With those wonderful breasts dangling in front of her face, Maxine imagined she already knew what heaven was like. Heaven had to be a place with two giant breasts waiting there to greet you, with well-defined nipples and a collective softness that begged for the chance to nurture and comfort. *Yes, indeed*, Maxine thought. *Heaven will have big breasts there waiting for me someday.*

As Betina slowly lowered herself onto Maxine's eager body, she smiled down at her and then sighed heavily as Maxine's tongue showed its appreciation and outlined a nipple before taking it into her warm, moist mouth.

"Oh, baby," Betina cooed. "Tell me where you're taking me tomorrow for Valentine's Day."

"It's a surprise," Maxine said, slipping her hand inside Betina's panties. "But something you've always wanted to do."

Betina's smile was slow and playful. "Did your friend with the helicopter come through this time?"

"Uh . . . no," Maxine said. "I'm still working on that one. This is something else, but it's a surprise." She found her lover to be very wet and continuing to coo. Betina lay on her side and opened her legs automatically as Maxine kissed her. That was one of the things Maxine loved most about her—the way Betina was constantly ready to make love no matter what the circumstances were or where the two of them happened to be. Sex was more than a longing or craving or a bodily response. For Betina sex seemed to be the very essence of who she was—a primal need no different than eating or breathing. Everything she did and everything she said held a hint of sensuality laced with humor and a dash of theatrics. In her profession as a board certified hair colorist, cosmetologist, and barber, male clients were fascinated by her, and she could make them look their best in no time. On the other hand, most straight women tried hard to dislike her, but Betina was personable and disarmingly clever and down to earth. She had what some referred to as charisma. There was no way to explain what exactly it was that drew people to her, but everyone who knew her had to admit that Betina had a *something* that could not be denied. Dr. Maxine Weston had recognized it right away and in the beginning, had set out to learn as much as she could.

Opening her legs further, Betina whispered, "Am I wet?"

"You're always wet."

"Just for you, baby," Betina said. She pulled Maxine's head to her breasts and Maxine found a nipple.

Remembering that the blinds in their bedroom were open, Maxine felt a new surge of arousal.

Betina worked at getting Maxine undressed while keeping her fingers busy between Betina's legs. The two of them were perfect for each other and made a conscious effort to keep their sexual exploits as safe and exciting as possible. Maxine was certain there wasn't a neighbor within a four-house radius of them who didn't have a telescope focused on their bedroom most evenings. Their blinds were always open and lights were usually on whenever they made love, and as a result they had *very* friendly neighbors. Maxine and Betina weren't promiscuous per se, just uninhibited about showing off their bodies. They didn't care who saw them or what sort of pleasure anyone else derived from what the two of them did together. They were only there to please each other. Everyone else was on their own.

In a voice thick with arousal as she squeezed her legs together trapping Maxine's fingers inside, Betina asked, "If we're not doing it in a helicopter, then what's my surprise?"

Maxine eased her fingers in and out and renewed a gentle stroking as she nuzzled Betina's neck. "If I tell you now it won't be a surprise." She kissed her throat and bare shoulder. "But we'll be up in the air while we're doing it. How does that sound?"

Chapter Two

It was unseasonably warm for February—even for south Texas—and Maxine knew this would work to her advantage. She took off early on Valentine's Day and made all the necessary arrangements. Dealing with carnival people wasn't quite the experience she had hoped it would be, but Maxine understood better than most how money could make things happen. Eventually she got what she wanted.

"Wear loose clothing, honey," Maxine said into her cell phone on her way home that afternoon. "Something that I can get you in and out of easily, okay?" She laughed at what she was asking Betina to do. Maxine always tried the *please be ready when I get home* line, but it never worked. Betina would promise to be dressed and ready when Maxine got there, but inevitably she would have on underwear and high heels and little else, while going from closet to closet looking for something to wear. This time proved to be no exception. When Maxine got home, that's exactly what she found.

"Something loose," Maxine reminded her. "We won't have a lot of space to work with."

"Is it the elevator in the Tower of the Americas?" Betina asked excitedly. "You know I've always wanted to do it there."

"No," Maxine said, making a mental note about the elevator in the Tower of the Americas. *That would be fun*, she thought. *Paradoxical sex on an elevator—going up while going down.*

Betina began dragging new outfits from the closet with a great deal of enthusiasm and animation. "Then where *are* you taking me!?" she gleefully asked.

Maxine had made reservations at a nice French restaurant where they flirted outrageously with each other as well as the gay waiter. By the time dinner was over, Betina was more than ready for her surprise.

"Soon," Maxine promised. "Very soon."

After dinner they took a ride out to the east side through a seedy area of town. Maxine could tell by the restless way Betina kept flouncing in her seat that she was getting impatient. Teasing her and making her wait this way was part of the tension-building phase Maxine enjoyed.

As they arrived at their destination, Betina said, "This is the fairgrounds to the rodeo." Her nose curled up a little, revealing the distaste she felt for her surroundings. Maxine laughed and winked at her.

"Please tell me you didn't get me rodeo tickets for Valentine's Day."

"Would I do something like that?" Maxine queried. "There's also a carnival on the fairgrounds, lover. With a giant Ferris wheel."

Betina's eyes lit up and she let out a squeal. "Ohmigod! We're gonna do it on the Ferris wheel? Like I wanted to do with Carolyn Hill in high school?"

"Only better," Maxine said. "You'll be doing it with me, and I know a whole lot more than Carolyn Hill ever did."

Betina leaned closer to her in the seat of the Jaguar and put her head on Maxine's shoulder. The traffic was backed up and Maxine could see nothing but taillights for miles. When they finally got to the entrance to the fairgrounds, Maxine smiled as Betina looped their arms together, but still kept her head on Maxine's shoulder.

"Is there anything you want to do first?" Maxine asked when they finally parked where the flag man pointed. "Get a corn dog? A candy apple? Check out the show barn?"

Betina moved back over to her side of the car and said, "Take me to the Ferris wheel, baby. I've waited twenty years for this."

Maxine laughed then set the parking brake. "We have one other stop to make first."

There were literally thousands of people as far as Maxine could see. The fairgrounds were alive with cowboys and cowgirls of all ages and sizes, most sporting new outfits that likely wouldn't be worn again the rest of the year. The crowd meandered through the stock show exhibits in huge steel barns, while taking breaks from the carnival on the other side of the Coliseum. Maxine got a whiff of manure in the air, mixed with the smoke from a *fajita* pit nearby. Betina held her hand so they wouldn't get separated from each other in the crowd.

"It's this way," Maxine said as she led the way toward the carnival and the haunted house. When they got there, Maxine spoke to the operator of the ride and reminded him of their earlier arrangement.

"Will I like this?" Betina asked as she gingerly stepped into the little two-person car that would take them into the dark tunnel of horrors. It looked as though they would be the only customers on the ride, but then two teenage couples bought tickets before things got underway.

Maxine laughed. "Sure you'll like it. Trust me."

There was a string of nine cars, each one several feet away from the others and easily separated by the twists and turns of the dark tunnel itself. Maxine and Betina were seated in one of the middle cars, while the other two couples were at opposite ends of the little train. As soon as the cars began to move, Betina giggled and gripped Maxine's hand.

The moment they rounded the first corner, an eerie red light flashed in front and to the side of them, revealing a Frankenstein mannequin with outstretched arms and a pasty green glow to his skin. Maxine put her arm around Betina and pulled her closer. She kissed her to the drone of bad pipe organ music, and then put her hand on Betina's right breast. Maxine could hear the sudden intake of breath and then that marvelous purring sound Betina always made when she was unexpectedly aroused.

"Oh, baby," Betina whispered, and then opened her legs.

Maxine knew that just around the next corner would be the headless man with the ax, and that the car they were riding in would stop as previously arranged with the attendant. Earlier in the day Maxine had taken this ride alone and afterward had told the operator what she wanted to have happen this evening. Right on cue, the car stopped just before the next gruesome tableau was completely revealed. Another faint glow of a red light gave them a sense of being alone, yet not really alone.

"Who loves you?" Maxine whispered as she kissed Betina's neck with hot, searing urgency.

"You do," Betina answered. "You. Oh, God. You, baby."

Maxine could hear voices behind them mixed in with the hokey organ music. She could also hear the teens in the car ahead of them asking each other why they were stopped.

"And who does it better for you?" Maxine whispered.

"No one, baby. No one does me like you do. No one."

"That's right," Maxine said against Betina's hair and ear. She could feel Betina tremble in her arms and then her legs opened even wider, silently begging for attention. Their kisses were wild now and laced with passion and longing. Maxine didn't want to get her too worked up just yet. Making love in the haunted house wasn't part of the plan. Maxine had it in mind to treat this more like haunted-house foreplay, something to get Betina primed and ready for the Ferris wheel later.

The tiny cars started moving again and the grumbling of the teens in the back car finally subsided.

"Baby," Maxine whispered after a short while, "the ride's almost over. We'll be coming out soon."

They had been too busy with each other to see the Abominable Snowman, Lizzie Borden and those pesky flying bats that had grazed Maxine's hair when she had been there earlier in the day.

"And how do you expect me to walk now?" Betina asked. "We need to go around this thing again."

Maxine leaned her head back and laughed. "No, I don't think so."

"Please? I want you, Maxie."

"I know you do. That's part of the plan."

Reaching for Maxine's hand, Betina placed it on her breasts where hard nipples pressed through her blouse.

"Watch it," Maxine warned. "You could put somebody's eye out with one of those things."

Once they were exiting the haunted house's tiny car, Maxine felt like they were two salmon swimming upstream as they fought through the crowd. Maxine held her lover's hand on their way to the Ferris wheel. She could tell Betina was still aroused by the way she intentionally let her right breast rub against Maxine's upper arm. They arrived at the Ferris wheel where the line was incredibly long. Maxine waved and got the operator's attention. He smiled and nodded back. To Maxine's relief, the man remembered her and motioned for them to move up to the front of the line.

Earlier that day Maxine had spent the good part of an hour nego-tiating a price for renting the Ferris wheel for a twenty-minute stretch of time. The operator informed her she had to buy every seat available for what was equivalent to nearly two rides per seat. In addition to that, the operator wanted two hundred dollars from her in order to make the Ferris wheel go the speed Maxine wanted.

12

"I've been looking for you," the man said as he helped them into their seats. He wore baggy gray pants and a red flannel shirt. The tobacco in his corncob pipe smelled like cherries. It reminded Maxine of her grandfather. Pipe smokers always evoked warm childhood memories for Maxine.

As she and Betina got into their seats, the operator lowered the security bar that kept them safely in place, and then put up a sign informing the rest of the crowd that it would be twenty more minutes before the next rides began. The groans and boos that followed only served to make Betina giggle more.

"In just a few minutes we should be the only ones on this thing," Maxine informed her. She noticed Betina's face was still flushed from their haunted house encounter. "Happy Valentine's Day, my love."

Betina leaned over and kissed her as the Ferris wheel slowly sent them up backward just a little bit higher while it unloaded other riders whose turns had ended.

"This thing is definitely in the way," Betina commented with a thump on the security bar that was across their laps.

"You think so?"

Maxine's trial spin on the Ferris wheel earlier in the day had helped with her decision to insist they wear loose clothing. It was the only way this would be a successful adventure.

"We'll have to see about that," Maxine said. She reached over and unbuttoned the top three buttons on Betina's shirt while undoing her own with the other hand. Betina's giggle made Maxine work faster on the buttons.

By the time the operator had stopped them at the very top position on the wheel, Maxine had both of their shirts unbuttoned. Betina's face was buried in Maxine's breasts with a hard nipple in her mouth, while Maxine worked her fingers up Betina's skirt where she found that Betina wasn't wearing any underwear. Maxine slid a finger in and out of her, beginning with first one and then three. Maxine could tell that her lover was close to coming by the way Betina stopped sucking Maxine's breast and threw her head back and began a series of "oh babies" until she was practically screaming. When she finally came, Betina showered Maxine's face with kisses and then returned to worshipping Maxine's breasts again.

As with most of their public sexual outings, it wasn't so much what they did to each other, but more importantly where they ended up doing it. Lengthy sessions of hot, sweaty sex could be accomplished at home, and very often were, but when they were out and about and engaged in more daring versions of their desire for each other, the intensity of an orgasm was solely derived from the fearless audacity of their actions. And it never failed to surprise Maxine how willing third parties were to accommodate their requests, no matter how scandalous or outrageous she and Betina wanted to be. At that very moment, Maxine loved imagining the crowd below watching them and nudging each other in the ribs as they pointed up at the Ferris wheel. It also made her hot and wet knowing that Betina was thinking and wanting the same thing. There was no limit to what two women with vivid imaginations and such an intense desire for each other could do.

"A little more, baby," Betina said as she urged Maxine to lean back as far as possible. "That's it."

Maxine loved the way Betina touched her when time and space were at a premium. They knew how to please each other in almost any situation or location, and could get right to the point at a moment's notice. A fleeting thought flashed in Maxine's head as she imagined sharing this story with her best friend, Elaine Marcaluso, at breakfast. *She'll never believe Betina had her hand in my pants on a carnival ride*, she thought with a chuckle.

She and Betina had one set of friends who would make them promise not to have sex while they were out with them, and another set of friends who kept in touch just to hear about their newest wanton acts of social disgrace. Maxine imagined she and Betina were the source of amusement to many, and were envied by a few, but no one who knew them could deny their love for sex and adventure.

Maxine came just as the Ferris wheel slowly began to move again.

14

Betina's fingers played her like a master musician, strumming her and kissing her until Maxine's loud moans finally turned into whimpers. Maxine was limp and spent as the Ferris wheel took its sweet time bringing them to the end of their glorious ride. Maxine laughed and snuggled delightedly in between Betina's breasts while they both attempted to fix their clothing.

"That was such a rush, lover," Betina said. "This is the best Valentine's Day ever."

"Ever?"

Betina nodded as she finished buttoning her blouse. "Ever."

"It's not over with yet."

The Ferris wheel brought them to the starting point where they faced a crowd of impatient people still waiting in line. Maxine smiled and as a bonus for a job well done, she pressed an additional twenty into the operator's hand after he released them from the security bar. The line for the Ferris wheel was much longer now, but only a few people gave them puzzled looks as Maxine and Betina exited the ride area. As they walked away, Maxine noticed that familiar flush on Betina's lovely face, which was always a clear sign of a recent sexual encounter.

"What would you like to do now?" Maxine asked while making their way through the crowded fairgrounds.

"You really want to know?"

Maxine reached for her hand and held it. "Of course I really want to know. It's Valentine's Day. I want to make things as special as possible for us."

Betina squeezed Maxine's hand and then let go. "You already have," she said quietly. "You never fail to surprise or amaze me. The sex is incredible, and it always has been with you. From the very first time we were together."

Maxine had to agree with that even though she didn't say so right then. There had been many times when she had wanted to thank Beina for saving her from a mundane life. Career-wise Maxine was set. Her medical practice was very successful and she was making more money than she could ever spend. But it was Betina who challenged her. Betina who intrigued her. Betina who had stolen her heart and kept her always wanting more, wanting something newer, something more daring, something hot and erotic. Betina had unleashed Maxine's passion and managed to keep her constantly hovering on the edge. Maxine often wondered if meeting Betina had been the turning point in her life. In the past, Maxine firmly believed that lovers were like stepping stones on the path to something bigger and better—but for her, Betina was everything she had always wanted.

Like a lightning bolt from a dark, menacing sky, someone plowed into them, stumbling and laughing. Maxine was brought back to the present by the jolt and the splat of a beer cup hitting the ground.

"Excuse me, ma'am," the cowboy said. "Did I get any on you? Hey! It's *you*! The nurse at the car wreck yesterday!"

Maxine recognized the hubcap-sized belt buckle first. "Hi," she said.

"She's the one I was tellin' you about," he said to the woman beside him. "She just *took* over and saved a buncha lives!"

"And she's *not* a nurse, by the way!" Betina said indignantly.

"It's okay, baby," Maxine whispered.

"Twenty years of schooling and he calls you a *nurse*?"

"Shhh. It's okay."

The cowboy tipped his hat and gave them his best drunken smile. "It's artificial resuscitation," he said as he carefully pronounced each word. "Not insemination." He wagged a finger at Maxine and smiled once more. "I won't make that mistake again." The cowboy put his arm around his girlfriend and waved at them. "See you around!"

Maxine got Betina walking with the crowd again.

"A nurse," Betina grumbled.

Maxine chuckled. "It's okay. So where were we?"

"I don't remember."

"You were about to tell me what you wanted to do for the rest of the evening," Maxine said. "We're all dressed up. What would you like to do?"

"We could go dancing," Betina suggested with renewed enthusiasm.

"Is there a bar in town we haven't been thrown out of yet for lewd acts on a dance floor?"

"There's a new boy's bar downtown," Betina said as she looped her arm through Maxine's again. "Joey told me about it. They don't know us there yet."

"Then dancing it is."

Betina put her head on Maxine's shoulder. "But we have to do something else first."

"I know. I was thinking the same thing."

"The backseat should work nicely. I love the way you throw your leg over the seat when I—"

"Could we walk a little faster while we talk about this?" Maxine asked.

They laughed all the way to the car.

Chapter Three

Maxine was late as usual. She wasn't sure whether it had been the shower with Betina that morning or the traffic jam on the interstate that had been the culprit this time. She parked her car beside Elaine's in the parking lot at Jim's Coffee Shop. Elaine was at their usual table talking on her cell phone when Maxine arrived. She put the phone away just as Maxine sat down.

"Good morning, Dr. Marcaluso," Maxine said while sliding into the booth.

"Good morning, Dr. Weston. That was my mother on the phone wondering if you can work at the clinic again next month. She's trying to put a schedule together."

"Hmm," Maxine said. "Let me talk to Woody today and see what his schedule looks like. I'll get back to your mother this afternoon."

They both reached for menus at the same time. Dr. Elaine Marcaluso was Maxine's oldest and dearest friend. They first met over a cadaver in a gross anatomy class at the School of Medicine at Stony Brook on Long Island. Even though back then they were classmates and politically active in the gay/lesbian organization on campus, they had never been lovers. Early on in their friendship, Maxine and Elaine never seemed to be single at the same time. As they continued on through the rigors of medical school and narrowed down their individual interests in medicine, their friendship became too important to risk jeopardizing over sex. Back in those days they spent a lot of time talking about medicine and women as well as their own personal likes and dislikes. Their first year in New York they studied together and shared everything. Many of their peers even viewed them as a couple. The only rough spot during their friendship, however, occurred when Maxine and Elaine went to Elaine's hometown in San Antonio. Elaine had arranged for them to do an away-rotation as an elective during their fourth year of medical school. They stayed with Elaine's family for the month and during that time, Maxine ended up sleeping with Elaine's younger sister, Mickey.

Elaine didn't find out about it until after they returned to New York. She was furious, hurt, and disappointed, but Maxine took full responsibility for her actions and continued apologizing for days and days until she was hoarse. Elaine's anger eventually subsided, but even now, nearly ten years later, it was still something that could set the usually mild-mannered Dr. Elaine Marcaluso off into a snippy fit of indignation. It was a subject they agreed not to talk about, but occasionally it slipped into a conversation.

Maxine closed her menu and slid it behind the napkin dispenser. "I don't even know why I look at that. I always order the same thing."

"It gives us the illusion of having choices," Elaine said. "Say, you've got a new hair color! It looks good!"

Maxine touched the top of her head where her short hair was spiked toward the back. Betina had given her a mauve color this time. Maxine insisted on having a low maintenance haircut since she was on the go so much of the time. Having a hair stylist for a lover kept her looking fashionable.

"What did you and Cheryl do for Valentine's Day?" Maxine asked.

The waitress came over and took their orders.

"We went out for a romantic dinner, then spent a few hours at a club on the River Walk that had a great blues band. Did you have the night off?"

"Are you kidding? Betina would've had my head on a platter if I hadn't arranged to be off. We went to the carnival at the rodeo."

Elaine chuckled. "For real?"

"Yes, for real. Foreplay in the haunted house and then sex on the Ferris wheel."

"For the love of Peter, Maxine," Elaine said with what was equivalent to a feminine snort. "Are you out of your mind? Attendance records are being broken every night there because of the mild weather! The radio said there were twenty thousand people there last night!"

"And most of them were in line at the Ferris wheel watching another kind of show."

Elaine shook her head in amazement while the waitress whizzed by leaving their coffees.

"But that wasn't even the best part," Maxine said. She made a secret bet with herself about how far she would get into the next part of her story before Elaine declined to hear any more. It was a little game they liked to play with each other.

"There's more? Sex on the Ferris wheel wasn't enough?"

"Oh, yes. There's more."

"You are the sickest puppy in the litter, Dr. Weston," Elaine said with a laugh. "And I mean that in a good way."

Maxine poured cream into her coffee and stirred it slowly. "After the Ferris wheel, we went back to the car and got in the backseat. That little dabbling in the haunted house just got Betina squirmy, but the lovemaking on the Ferris wheel got her really ready."

"Why weren't there police officers waiting for you when the ride was over?"

"And what a ride it was," Maxine said wistfully.

"I still don't understand how you two get away with such things."

"Human nature, Dr. Marcaluso," Maxine said philosophically. "Americans are voyeurs at heart. They're so anal in their own lives and belief systems that they need something extra to get them going. That's why porn stars make more than teachers or health care providers. Most Americans have no idea how to get in touch with themselves, so to speak. In a way, Betina and I perform a service not only to each other, but members of the public as well. We inspire them to carry on with our traditions."

"Oh, give me a break," Elaine said with a classic eye roll.

Maxine threw her head back and laughed. She loved teasing her incredibly-vanilla-dermatologist friend this way. "I still haven't even gotten to the good part yet."

"At least tell me you weren't naked on the Ferris wheel."

"Loose clothing was the key to that endeavor being a success."

"Wasn't it cold up there at the top? The weather's been nice, but it's still February."

"We didn't give the weather another thought."

"Okay, so after the Ferris wheel incident, then what happened? Or do I even want to know?"

With the hint of a smile, Maxine said, "It's obvious to me that you want to know."

"I'm just making conversation until my breakfast arrives," Elaine declared. "You think I don't understand how this process works? Part of this exhibitionism persona you have not only involves having sex in public places, but it then spills over into your everyday life and how you enjoy telling others about it."

"So humor me and let me finish my story."

Elaine smiled and shook her head. "Like I could stop you. Go ahead. I'll let you know when I've had enough."

"We got back to the car and Betina was all over me. We're in the

21

backseat getting our clothes off and I can hear people close to the car. Some were walking past us on their way to the fairgrounds and carnival area, and some were just standing nearby talking. Well, you know how Betina gets when we're around people that way."

"I didn't receive a phone call to bail you out of jail last night," Elaine said dryly, "so I'm assuming things went as planned."

"They went quite well, as a matter of fact. Let's just say the louder Betina got as we continued on into sexual bliss, the more quiet it became outside the car. At one point it seemed as though we were the only people there in that gigantic parking lot. I bet that particular parking lot alone covered about ten acres. Anyway, afterward we're giggling and kissing in the backseat, sorting through our clothes that were strewn all over the car. Oh, that reminds me. I need to make sure my shocks are all okay. We gave my car a good workout and I think I heard squeaking. A sixty-thousand-dollar car shouldn't be squeaking that way."

"Oh, puhleeze," Elaine said as she rolled her eyes again and tried to suppress a chuckle.

Maxine laughed at Elaine's theatrics. "As I was saying," she continued, "we got dressed again, and I can't emphasize enough how important it is to wear baggy clothing when you do something like this."

"You're wasting that speech on me, I'm afraid."

"Anyway," Maxine said, "we put ourselves back together again and then I got out of the car so I could get in the front seat to drive. We'd decided earlier to go dancing at a gay bar downtown. So I got out of the car and I saw about eight cowboys there behind us on the next row over. They were pretending to be interested in a pickup, but they couldn't take their eyes off me."

Elaine shook her head.

"I think one of them accidentally swallowed some snuff he had packed in his bottom lip when he saw Betina get out of the backseat, though. He started coughing and choking. His buddies were there to slap him on the back a few times. No doubt he expected one of us to be a man."

"No doubt," Elaine said. "You enjoyed all of that, didn't you?"

"Every hot, incredible moment," Maxine confirmed. "Should I continue and tell you what happened at the bar?"

"I don't believe this! There's more?"

"There's always more," Maxine said. "We got to the bar and met Betina's brother and friends there. We were the only women in the entire place, so we had the ladies room all to ourselves for a while. We got out on the dance floor after a while and did a little bumping and grinding. All that was wasted on gay men, though. No one gave us another look," she said with a laugh, "so it wasn't as much fun as it could have been until we saw a straight couple come in."

"What was a straight couple doing there?"

"Joey said they go there all the time to try and pick up someone for a threesome. They never get any takers, but they are regulars there, I guess."

"Eww," Elaine said with a crinkled nose.

"I agree. They'd have better luck running an ad in the classifieds. But after a while, the couple seemed to like watching Betina and me dance together, so that was fun." With another smile, Maxine added, "Betina and I get into it more when we have an audience."

"Yeah, yeah. I know. So was that it?"

"I just have one more thing to add," Maxine said. The waitress brought their orders and set the wrong plates down in front of them. Maxine and Elaine exchanged plates and got settled again.

"What else happened?" Elaine asked. "You two didn't get propositioned again, did you?"

"Oh, no. We try and make it obvious we only like being with each other."

Elaine handed her the salt and pepper without being asked.

"It was the kiss Betina gave me when we went into the bathroom together." Maxine set the pepper shaker down as the memory of that kiss came back to her again.

"What kind of kiss was it?" Elaine asked.

In a voice laced with a husky seriousness, Maxine said, "No one's ever kissed me that way before. She sort of pushed me against the wall and grabbed a handful of my hair on the back of my head. She kissed me so hard it made my knees weak." She looked across the table at Elaine and said, "They're weak all over again right now just from describing it."

"Wow," Elaine said. "Your whole voice just changed."

"Has anyone ever made you feel that way with a kiss?"

"Yes. The first time Cheryl kissed me."

"I felt like I was on fire," Maxine said. "So anyway, that was how we spent our Valentine's Day. Now tell me about that little blues band you mentioned on the River Walk."

Maxine gave Elaine's mother, Blanche Marcaluso, a call to set up a day in March for her to volunteer at the free clinic downtown. Blanche was a nurse and the administrator for the clinic. She knew enough doctors to keep the clinic staffed with volunteers on next to no budget. Maxine and Elaine were often asked to donate more time than most of the other physicians Blanche either knew or worked with mainly because she knew them better and shared their interests in helping the indigent population.

"I can give you eight hours on the third Thursday in March," Maxine said. "That third Saturday in the morning looks good, too. Let's say eight till five."

"Thank you, Maxine," Blanche said. "I'll start lining up patients for you right away."

"I'm happy to be your pap smear slave. How's Phoebe doing?"

"Her allergies are kicking up," Blanche said. "This warm weather has something in the air that doesn't agree with her."

"Plant sperm, aka pollen, is not our friend."

Blanche laughed. "What an interesting way to put it."

"Have her put a little Vaseline just inside the nose. It'll help catch some of it. You and Phoebe will have to come over for dinner some night."

24

"We'd like that!"

"I'll have Betina call you."

As soon as she hung up, her receptionist Mona knocked on Maxine's office door. Mona was young and spunky, with short black hair and a bright patch of purple near her bangs that Betina was totally responsible for. Mona had been toying with the idea of getting the purple highlight for nearly six months before Betina dared her to do it. So far it had been touched up twice already.

"Patricia Keller called," Mona said. "Her water broke. She's on the way to the hospital."

Patricia Keller, Maxine thought. *She's on time.*

"How many are still waiting out front?" Maxine asked.

"Three in the waiting room and one in the chute."

Maxine laughed. Mona's boyfriend was a bronc rider in town for the rodeo. To a regular rodeo fan, having "one in the chute" referred to a cowboy perched on a wild horse or bull in the pen just before they opened the gate to let them out. But to Mona and Maxine, "one in the chute" meant a patient waiting for her in the stirrups.

"Reschedule the patients in the waiting room and tell the hospital I'll be there in twenty minutes."

Chapter Four

Maxine was tired as she opened the garage door with the remote and drove her car inside. She could see a dim light on in the kitchen and a lamp burning in the living room—like two beacons welcoming her home. Once Maxine got inside the house, she noticed it was well after midnight already. She had been on her feet for nearly five hours. The Keller delivery had been a lengthy one, and Maxine had an early day in the morning with another full schedule of patients to take care of.

She switched off the lamp in the living room and found her way through the dark sprawling house to the master bedroom. Maxine had taken a shower at the hospital so she'd be awake enough to drive home. After quietly taking off her clothes and putting her pager on the nightstand, she slipped into the king-size bed and liked the way the cool, silky sheets felt against her skin.

"Is that you?" Betina asked in a sleepy voice.

Maxine managed a tired smile. "Who else were you expecting, lover?" They met in the center of the bed. Betina's warm, naked body felt good against Maxine's.

"A boy or a girl?" Betina asked sleepily. She pulled Maxine into her arms and kissed the top of her head.

"A boy. Mother and baby are doing fine." She sank deeper into Betina's arms and adored lying with her this way. Betina always smelled so good and had to be the softest woman Maxine had ever known.

"Are you hungry?" Betina asked.

"I'm too tired to eat."

"Poor baby," Betina cooed. She kissed Maxine's forehead and hugged her. "Tomorrow's St. Patrick's Day. Joey wants us to dress up like leprechauns." She yawned and gave Maxine an extra squeeze. "I think he just wants an excuse to wear green tights."

Maxine smiled and rubbed her cheek against Betina's shoulder. "How was your day?" she asked, but they were both asleep before Betina could get out a coherent sentence.

Three hours later, Maxine heard the beeping and disentangled herself from Betina's embrace. Betina rolled over and tugged on the covers as Maxine reached for her pager and got out of bed. She fumbled for the cordless phone in the dark and scooped up her pager on the way to the bathroom. She turned on the light and squinted against its harsh intrusion. Once she could focus properly, Maxine saw the digital numbers on her pager, then dialed the number to her answering service.

"This is Dr. Weston returning a page."

"Dr. Weston, you have an emergency call from a Gordon Langston."

"Can you transfer me?"

"Yes, ma'am. One moment please."

Maxine put a towel on the edge of the huge bathtub and sat

down. She had no desire to have her naked butt come into direct contact with cold porcelain. She ran her fingers through her hair and tried to focus on the clock on the wall. It was three in the morning. She could hear the phone ringing on the other end. *Harriet Langston,* she thought. *She's in her third trimester. She's not due for another eight weeks.*

"Hello?" a male voice said on the other end.

"This is Dr. Weston. What seems to be the problem, Gordon?"

"Thank you for calling back so quickly," he said. Maxine could hear the tension in his voice. She had met him once when he accompanied his wife on her first visit to Maxine's office. The Langstons were in their early forties and had been trying to conceive for ten years. This was their first child and so far there had been no complications.

"My wife was in a car accident earlier this evening," he said. "They took her to the hospital as a precaution and everything seemed fine. They released her a few hours ago and told us if there was a problem, we should contact her OB physician. Then about twenty minutes ago she started bleeding, so I called you."

Maxine stood up and left the bathroom, keeping the door cracked just enough to let some light into the bedroom.

"You did the right thing, Gordon," Maxine said quietly into the phone. "Is there any cramping?" She could hear him asking his wife the question.

"No," he said.

"Okay. Good. Take her to the emergency room at the Methodist Hospital. I'll meet you there and we'll see what's going on."

"Thank you."

Maxine turned the phone off and found some clean clothes to wear. Betina had a sports bag pre-packed and ready for her inside the closet so Maxine would have something to wear to work in the morning if she didn't make it back home in time to change.

"Another baby on the way?" came Betina's sleepy voice from the bed.

"I hope not," Maxine said. She pulled on a pair of black pants and sat on the edge of the bed to put her socks and shoes on. "She's not due for another eight weeks." Maxine tugged on a sports bra and then buttoned up her shirt. She clipped her pager to the waistband of her pants and was ready to go. She had a brush in the car and would make herself more presentable on the way to the hospital.

"Give your baby a kiss before you go," Betina said.

Maxine smiled and crawled onto the bed. Betina put her arms around Maxine's neck and gave her a warm, sleepy kiss.

"Who loves you?" Maxine whispered.

"You love me."

"I'll probably go back to the office and get some sleep there if it's too late to come home."

Betina kissed her again. "Don't forget to call Elaine about breakfast if you can't make it."

"Thanks for reminding me," Maxine said. She slipped out of Betina's embrace and grabbed her sports bag and went to search for her keys.

Maxine barely heard the light knock on her office door the following morning. Every time she had to sleep in her office, she was extremely grateful that Betina had taken her shopping for a comfortable futon.

Mona stuck her head in the door. "You decent?"

"I have clothes on, if that's what you mean," Maxine said sleepily.

"Thanks for the note this morning telling us where you were," Mona said.

Maxine chuckled then stretched the early-morning kinks from her body.

"Here's some coffee and a bagel," Mona said. "Chop-chop. Your first patient will be in the chute in fifteen minutes."

Maxine groaned and opted for a shower. She needed to be awake and a bit more professional looking in the course of fifteen minutes.

She tossed the blanket off and got up. Taking her coffee and gym bag with her down the hall to the office bathroom, she mumbled a greeting to her nurse as they passed each other. Maxine was the only one to ever use the shower in the office, so her personal toiletries were all lined up there on the small shelf inside the shower. She unzipped the gym bag and pulled out two clean towels, a clean bra and underwear, clean socks, a starched pair of olive-drab cargo pants and a thin yellow turtleneck sweater. Stuck to the underwear was a large yellow Post-it with the words "Betina loves you" written on it. Maxine smiled and touched the note to her lips.

It had been a long day, but Maxine managed to see all of her patients and even check in on Harriet Langston at the hospital. After discharging her, Maxine was finally on her way home. She called the house and got Betina on the second ring.

"Are you stuck in traffic, baby?" Betina asked.

"No. Not at all. I'll be there in about five minutes."

"I picked up a movie for us to watch later," Betina said. "Well, for me to watch and for you to sleep through."

"Now, what kind of thing is that to say?"

They both laughed. Being notorious for sleeping through them, Maxine hadn't seen a complete movie in years.

"What's for dinner?" Maxine asked.

"Your favorite. Oven-fried chicken and biscuits, Betina's green beans and an acorn squash casserole thingy I'm throwing together as we speak."

"It sounds fabulous. I'll be home in a few."

Maxine put her cell phone away and checked her pager out of habit. An evening at home was exactly what she needed. She liked the balance Betina gave her. There were times when Betina seemed to know when they needed to get out and do things with other people and then times when just being alone together at home was called for.

Maxine whipped into the garage and the door closed behind her car. She clipped the remote back on her visor and collected her purse and the gym bag she'd left with at three that morning. As soon as she got out of the car, Maxine could hear a ZZ Top CD playing in the house. She opened the door that led into the kitchen and dropped her gym bag beside the pantry.

"There you are!" Betina said as she held her arms open.

Maxine laughed at the words *I Kiss Better Than I Cook* etched on Betina's apron.

"Let's check this out," Maxine said. She took Betina into her arms and kissed her sweetly. "So far so good. It smells great in here."

"What did you have for lunch?"

"A huge salad that took me three hours to finish."

"How huge *was* that salad?" Betina asked with a wink. She gave Maxine a quick peck on the lips then went to check on the green beans.

"I had to finish it in between patients. It was a wildly busy day."

"How's Harriet Langston?"

"I sent her home this evening. I got the bleeding stopped, so she should be fine. I put her on bed rest for a week. How was your day?"

"Remember that guy I told you about last month who seemed to have a fondness for my breasts?" Betina said. She put the lid back on the pot of green beans then opened the oven to peek inside.

"The guy who liked leaning his head back to touch your chest?"

"That's the one!"

"So he had an appointment today? What happened?"

"He tried that again and it pissed me off. I must be PMSing. He leaned that balding head back and brushed against my girls and I whacked him with my comb before I even gave it a second thought."

Maxine chuckled. She loved how Betina had special names for certain parts of her body. Her breasts were fondly referred to as either "the girls" or "my girls" and her clitoris was simply called "she," as if it were a real person with "her" own personality and a life of its own.

"What did he say after you whacked him?"

"Nothing. Not much he could say. He knew what he was doing. Then I leaned in close to him and I said, 'You do that again, and I'll make sure that gay boy over there cuts your hair next time. He likes for guys to rub all over him.'"

"Ohmigod! Did you really say that?"

"You're danged right I did."

"Does Joey know what happened?"

"He does now. So we probably lost a client today, but I don't care. I don't need clients like that."

"Well, good for you! I'm proud of you."

"Just one person I want leaning into me," Betina said with a wink.

"Do I have time to lean before dinner?" Maxine asked as she nuzzled Betina's sweet-smelling neck.

"I'll make time for you, lover."

The last thing Maxine remembered was laying on the sofa with her head in Betina's lap. As she dozed off, Maxine was aware of Betina slipping her hand up inside her sweater, but neither that nor the movie were anything more than a vague memory now as Betina searched for the remote on the sofa.

"How was the movie?" Maxine asked sleepily. She still had her eyes closed. "Would I have liked it?"

Betina turned off the DVD player and laughed. "You might have. Did you get a good nap?"

Maxine loved the way Betina touched her hair when they were together this way. It was such an intimate, sensuous thing, and Maxine felt totally relaxed and at peace with her.

"When can we have some people over for dinner?" Maxine asked. "I spoke with Blanche yesterday. I'd like to see them again. She and Phoebe are a fun couple."

Betina once again slipped her hand under Maxine's sweater.

"Or we could meet them for dinner some night," Maxine added.

"I like having people over," Betina said. "When is Woody on call for you again?"

"I'll check tomorrow and let you know. We had to change the schedule."

Betina's hand moved up and covered Maxine's breast. Betina looked down at her and asked, "How sleepy are you?"

Maxine smiled and was amazed at how good she was beginning to feel. "Let me show you how awake I am."

"Which would you prefer? Making love here or in the bedroom?"

"Let's start out here."

Betina tilted her blond head back and laughed.

Chapter Five

Maxine couldn't remember a time when she felt more relaxed and more loved than she did at that very moment. The whole evening at home had been a constant string of pampering and attention to personal details. All Maxine had to do from the moment she arrived home was enjoy Betina's efforts to please her.

There were so many things about Betina that sparked Maxine's imagination and had eventually captured her heart. Their mutual interest in exhibitionism was like a bonus for Maxine. That side of her nature had been discovered with Betina's help, and it served as the kind of bond that Maxine would never have imagined possible.

Early during her first few months with Betina, she once confided to her friend Elaine, "I don't know what's bothering me more about this relationship. Is it the fact that she dreams up these outrageous things for us to do, or is it the fact that I'm so willing to do them *with* her?"

It took Maxine several more months to finally realize that she became as turned on and feverish over their public encounters as Betina did. Now that their fifth anniversary had come and gone already, Maxine felt as though she had known Betina her whole life.

"Tell me what you're thinking right now," Betina said with her hand casually placed under Maxine's sweater. Maxine's head was still in her lap and there was no other place she would rather be.

"I was thinking how nice this is."

"What in particular?"

Betina moved her hand up until she found Maxine's breast again.

"Coming home to you every night," Maxine said. "The way you take care of the little things for me. How you touch me. The way I feel when I'm with you."

Maxine noticed how the warmth spread through her body as Betina's fingers slowly coaxed her nipples into hard olive-shaped tokens of desire. The caresses were light but direct through the soft cotton fabric of her bra. Maxine absolutely adored being touched this way.

"That's a lot of thinking you've been doing," Betina said.

Maxine closed her eyes and rubbed her cheek against Betina's thigh. They both still had their clothes on, but Maxine was almost ready to remedy that situation.

"Right now I can't think of anything other than you and what your fingers are doing."

"Then my plan is working," Betina said. "Are you awake enough to enjoy the other things I have in mind for you?"

"When have you ever known me to sleep through this kind of attention?"

"Once after you delivered the Elliott triplets," Betina said as she slipped her hand inside Maxine's bra. "Then again after the burro ride at the Grand Canyon."

Maxine laughed. "You're actually keeping track?" She sat up and pulled the sweater over her head then did the same with the sports bra. "Besides, I still say the burro I had was suicidal. I was exhausted after spending the day terrified from teetering on the edge of that six-inch-wide trail."

With her breasts free, they seemed to have a mind of their own as her nipples puckered in anticipation of some much-needed attention. To Maxine's delight, Betina leaned closer and captured one with her hand and then her lips. Maxine always loved the way Betina kissed her nipples before taking them into her mouth. This time, however, she kissed each one and said, "Two times in five years is an admirable record, lover."

Betina then touched her tongue to Maxine's right nipple and took it into her mouth. Maxine felt a surge of heat race through her body only seconds before a series of moans escaped from her throat. They both knew that Maxine would come too quickly if Betina did much more than this over a short period of time, so it was their habit to feel, grope, and fondle each other while mostly staying dressed. Betina was multi-orgasmic, while Maxine seldom had more than one right away. For Maxine it was just as good for her to listen to Betina's eloquent string of "ooohhhs" as it was to have her face buried between Betina's legs as she rode her tongue to a very satisfying release. They complemented each other in this way. Betina's ability to achieve several orgasms quickly and steadily over a short period of time was one of the things that kept them so focused on sex. Maxine loved Betina's passion and her appreciation for making love. Betina's humor, generosity, tenderness, and sense of fun and adventure in everything she did were just added bonuses to an already incredible package.

Betina pulled her mouth away from Maxine's breasts and then kissed her. It was only then that Maxine remembered that the living room drapes and blinds were open, which meant old man Gardner across the street probably had his telescope zoomed in on them if his wife happened to be asleep already.

As they continued kissing, Maxine and Betina both worked at getting Betina out of her clothes. They were good at it, and were both naked in record time. Maxine always remembered Betina's one rule about making love when they were at home alone. "If *I'm* naked, then you're going to be naked." Betina often referred to it as the "Everybody Gets Naked" rule.

There was a built-in recliner at the end of the sofa where Betina was already sitting, so they made good use of that as well. Betina scooted further down and threw her right leg over its arm.

"For my birthday I want a recliner with stirrups," Betina said. "Have I mentioned that before?" Her fingertips touched Maxine's hair as Maxine kissed her way down Betina's stomach and then nibbled at the very edge of her crisp, blond triangle.

"Don't tease me," Betina said as she raised her hips to find Maxine's mouth.

Maxine smiled to herself, knowing full well that Betina loved being teased like this. The moment they seriously began to make love, Betina wouldn't care what else happened around them. The house could crumble and blow away a piece at a time, but as long as Maxine's mouth and tongue were fully engaged, nothing else mattered.

"Don't tease me," Betina said again in a husky whisper.

Maxine continued to kiss the inside of Betina's thighs and occasionally grazed her clitoris with the flick of a tongue. The more Betina begged not to be teased, the more Maxine teased her.

Then as if Maxine were the one who could no longer wait, she started down low and slowly brought her tongue up until she found Betina's small, hidden clit. The deep intake of breath Maxine heard from her, mixed with Betina's murmuring of the words, "Oh, baby," were just the beginning. Once official contact was made with Maxine's tongue, they were off in search of the first round of orgasmic bliss.

Betina was a screamer by nature, and the acoustics in their living room were well suited for their favorite pastime. When they made love in places where being quiet was either necessary or prudent, Betina became aroused more quickly, as if the struggle to maintain silence lent itself to passion instead. But when they were at home where time or discretion were no longer factors, there was more teasing and a relaxed atmosphere reflected in their actions. Maxine knew Betina's body as well as she knew her own. Even from the beginning, there had been very few questions about what felt good and what felt better. For Betina, it *all* seemed to feel good.

Maxine used the tip of her tongue to circle Betina's clit. She could feel it swelling with each choreographed flick. Sucking it into her mouth, Maxine thoroughly enjoyed the sounds Betina made, as well as the mere essence of making love to her this way.

"Is she out?" Betina asked in a breathless whisper, referring to the size of her clitoris at the moment.

Maxine moved her right hand to Betina's knee and gave it a firm squeeze. A signal they had worked out to communicate a yes or no response so Maxine wouldn't have to stop what she was doing, the brief knee squeeze was a definite "no" in answer to the question. Maxine had always found it amusing how Betina became so preoccupied with the status of her clitoris. If it didn't swell and "show itself" right away, she worried over its whereabouts. In the beginning, Maxine had taken the time to answer with a verbal yes or a no to Betina's never ending "Is she out?" question.

It was during their third time together at the very beginning of their relationship that Maxine took her tongue away long enough to ask a question of her own. "Does this feel good?" Maxine had asked.

"Ohmigod yes," Betina blurted.

"Then stop worrying about her being out."

"But *is* she out?"

In between sucking, licking, and overall coaxing, Maxine was able to say, "Uh . . . no. Not yet," before continuing on with what she was doing.

"Damn. Then where *is* she?!"

"Who cares where she is if it feels good?"

Finally after Betina came like a runaway train, Maxine was still amazed that the status of her clitoris was such a concern for her.

"How can you come that way and still worry about her being out or not?" Maxine later asked. She nestled into Betina's arms and nuzzled her ample breasts. Letting her hand stay cupped between Betina's legs, they finally had the time to discuss this clitoris obsession Betina had.

"Do you think your orgasms are better when she's out?" Maxine asked.

"Better?" Betina said. "Hmm. I don't know." Her throaty chuckle was such a nice sound to Maxine. "I can't imagine an orgasm better than that one. Mercy, lover. Even my worst orgasm with you was fabulous."

"Then if your orgasms are no better if she's out, it shouldn't matter what size she is."

Maxine's fingers slowly opened her up and slipped inside. Betina sighed heavily and spread her legs a little more.

"That feels so good."

Maxine smiled. "Does it?" she asked, knowing full well that Betina's body could continue feeling this way for as long as they wanted to make love.

"I think the reason it's important to me that she comes out," Betina said as she began a slow squirm against Maxine's caress, "is because I want her to show you how much she likes what you do to me. Coming out and making herself big and all hot and throbby is the least she can do under the circumstances."

"Is 'throbby' even a word?" Maxine asked as she licked one of Betina's nipples.

"It is now."

"Well," Maxine said. Her fingers were wet as she easily circled Betina's clitoris again. "Trust me, babe. She shows me all kinds of appreciation whether she's out or not."

That conversation had taken place nearly five years ago, and Betina still wanted reports on the in-and-out status of her clitoris when they made love. Now it was more of a habit than a necessity, but at the moment, Maxine was taking her time enjoying Betina's body and listening to her lover's soliloquy of encouragement as they both did their best to bring about the first of many orgasms to come throughout the evening.

Maxine did a quick probe a few inches lower before bringing the tip of her tongue back up again and swirling it around Betina's throbbing center. The quick intake of breath and the long, throaty moan reflected the heat and intensity of her actions. Then as if something new and elaborate had suddenly clicked in, Betina began to move against Maxine's mouth. She gently took Maxine's head in her hands and caressed her hair and ears as the urgency to have her closer seemed to take over.

"Ohh . . . please . . . ," Betina whispered breathlessly. Her legs were open and her fingers mingled wildly in Maxine's hair. "There, baby. Yes, yes, yes . . . there."

Maxine knew the rest was all downhill now. Betina would throw her head back and grind herself into Maxine's very willing lips, mouth, and tongue. However many orgasms would follow that night would be even more intense than this one. Once "she" was awake and activated, there was no stopping her until either sleep or exhaustion arrived.

"You do me so good, lover," Betina declared as she continued to quiver with Maxine's efforts to prolong the sensation for her. "Don't stop . . . please . . . don't stop."

Maxine had to chuckle to herself each time she heard Betina beg for her not to stop. *When have I ever stopped?* she wondered. *And not only that*, why *would I ever stop?*

In Maxine's mind this was what every lesbian lived for and searched for her entire life—someone who was the perfect match, both in and out of bed. Her incredible luck in finding this woman was still a mystery to her, but Maxine didn't fret over her good fortune. She just knew that she would do whatever it took to keep Betina and their relationship happy and safe.

"Oh, gawd it feels so good, Maxie. Don't stop . . . please . . . don't stop."

Maxie, Maxine thought. *I love it when she calls me that.* It never failed to make Maxine smile when she heard Betina say that name. When she used it in bed, it usually meant she was close to coming again.

Flattening out her tongue, Maxine once again probed a bit lower and then came back up with a nice swirling motion around Betina's swollen clitoris. As she continued this slow mixture of licking and sucking, she could hear Betina's constant pleas for her not to stop. Those impassioned words alone were enough to make Maxine wet and "throbby."

"Yes, baby . . . ," Betina cooed in a throaty whisper. "There . . . yes . . . just like that. There, there, there . . ."

She threw her head back again as her whole body began to tremble. "Yes, yes, yes, yes! Don't stop . . . please . . . don't stop!"

Maxine could feel her own swell of desire begin to take over as she listened to Betina's string of "ohmigods" vibrate through the living room. It was so easy to come with this woman. So very, very easy.

Chapter Six

Maxine checked the six-inch-long abdominal incision on her patient and liked the way it was healing. As she removed the staples, Maxine asked, "Have you had any bleeding?"

"No," the woman said as she made an effort to not look at what Maxine was doing.

After having performed a complete hysterectomy in addition to removing a grapefruit-sized, benign fibroid tumor, Maxine wished all of her patients were able to embrace that type of surgery with such positive energy. The courage of women in general continued to astound her, and their strength and humor were just a few of the things that helped provide a balance for some of the more unpleas-ant aspects of what Maxine faced each day.

"Any pain besides the expected soreness from the incision?"

"Not since I left the hospital," the woman said.

Luz Flores was a relatively new patient—a friend of a friend. Luz worked on the local lesbian paper where Maxine had recently submitted a series of articles on women's health issues. In her early forties, Luz's periods had been getting increasingly painful to the point where she was bedridden for several hours before it actually started each month. After getting the results of a sonogram, Luz had come to Maxine's office to discuss what needed to be done next.

"You have an abdominal mass that's causing the pain," Maxine had told her. "We need to go in and see what it is." After scanning a few documents in the file she had in front of her, Maxine looked up to meet Luz's worried expression. "There's a chance the mass is cancerous, and a better chance that you'll need at least a partial hysterectomy."

Maxine gave her a moment for everything to sink in before asking if she had any questions.

"Uh . . . ," Luz said. Her soft brown eyes were wide and teary. Maxine moved a small box of tissue closer to her. Luz's expression went from registering puzzled uncertainty to almost instant fear. Maxine knew both of those looks well.

"I've outlined the worst case scenario for you already," Maxine continued.

In a trembling voice, Luz said, "You mean the cancer?"

"Yes. The possibility of cancer. If you don't have the surgery, the pain will get worse before your periods begin each month."

"I'm not sure the pain *can* get worse," Luz said as she blew her nose. "I've never had pain like that before."

"It can be very intense," Maxine agreed, "and it can make ten minutes of doubling over seem like hours."

"That's so true," Luz said, clearing her throat. "What are the chances of the mass being cancerous?"

"Fifty-fifty," Maxine said honestly. Sugarcoating this information was not an option. Maxine wanted each of her patients to be prepared for bad news if that became the case. "I won't know until I get in there." She pulled a calendar closer and checked her schedule. "If you agree to have the surgery, I'd like to do it next Monday."

The surprise on Luz's face made her eyes widen even more. She nodded and sniffed.

"I might not have to take everything," Maxine said, "but again, I won't know until I get in there and see what we have."

"If you're going in there anyway, can you take it all?"

"I can if that's what you want."

"Yes. Take it all," Luz said, her voice trailing off.

"Some women like keeping the ovaries when at all possible."

Luz blew her nose. "Not me," she said. "I'm not using any of it anyway."

Maxine smiled and reached for her prescription pad. "I want you to check into the Methodist Hospital on Sunday evening by six. Is there someone who can help you with that?"

"Yes. My partner."

Maxine noticed that Luz's hands were shaking. She wanted to set her mind at ease, but also didn't want to make any promises she couldn't keep.

"While you're in there," Luz said, "can you snip my appendix? It can't be too far away from everything else you'll be fooling with."

Maxine shook her head and laughed. "No. I'm sorry. I can't do that."

"Fifty-fifty," Luz said under her breath. "My luck has never been very good."

"Then maybe that's about to change." Maxine tore off the prescription from the pad and handed it to her. "You can pick up a bottle of magnesium citrate at any pharmacy. It's an over-the-counter item. Take the whole bottle earlier in the day before you check into the hospital. No eating or drinking after midnight on Sunday evening." Maxine reached into her desk drawer and found the video she was looking for. "Watch this between now and then. It explains the surgery and might answer some of the questions you don't even realize you have yet. You can also call me if there's something that's not clear to you, or you can talk to me the morning of the surgery."

Luz took the video. Maxine noticed her hands were still shaking. "What's this for again?" Luz asked, waving the prescription.

"It's a saline laxative."

"Oh, joy."

For Maxine, the most interesting thing about this patient was how Luz Flores had prepared herself for the surgery. What should have been a frightening time in her life, filled with raw emotion and unprecedented fear, became just an ordinary day to Luz. On the morning of the surgery, Maxine went to her hospital room to see how she was doing. Luz was sitting up in bed with an IV in her arm, looking as though she might be waiting for her favorite television program to come on. An attractive woman about Maxine's height stood beside Luz, fussing with the thin thermal blanket on the bed.

"Good morning," Maxine said. "They'll be coming for you soon." To the woman by the bed, she said, "I'm Dr. Weston." She took a few moments to study her. After the surgery, Maxine would be looking for this woman in the waiting room to report on Luz's condition as well as the findings during surgery.

"Good morning," the woman said. She was a bit older than Luz, in her late forties. She wore a gray skirt and a pale pink blouse. Her voice was low and Maxine could see how nervous she was as she reached for Luz's hand.

"I have a few special requests," Luz said from the bed. "I went to a therapist and got hypnotized. I'm so chilled right now, it almost feels too weird to be here."

"I'm glad to see one of us is chilled," her partner said.

All three of them laughed. *Hypnosis*, Maxine thought. *Hmm. Interesting.*

Dressed in light gray scrubs and a white lab coat, Maxine stuck her hands in her pockets before asking, "What requests do you have?" They would be wheeling Luz to pre-op in a few minutes.

"The therapist who hypnotized me planted several suggestions," Luz said.

To Maxine, Luz Flores did not appear to be the one about to undergo major surgery, or who was facing possible cancer in her immediate future. She was relaxed and smiling and seemed to have a peacefulness about her that Maxine hadn't seen the other two times they had met. Luz's partner, however, kept touching Luz's hair and straightening the already smooth blanket on the bed.

"She planted suggestions about healing quickly and experiencing minimal bleeding," Luz continued. "She also wanted to make sure I didn't hear or remember anything that went on during the surgery."

"I see," Maxine said. She was in favor of anything that made a patient feel better, whether she personally believed in the methods used or not. The human mind was a very complex thing, and Maxine had been at this long enough to know when to embrace and encourage a more optimistic way of thinking.

"I can't even explain how positive I feel about the surgery," Luz said.

"So only one of us is a wreck at the moment," her partner said to Maxine.

One of the requests Luz had was for Maxine to call the therapist and give her feedback on the surgery and the amount of bleeding there had been. Maxine agreed to do it and slipped the therapist's business card into her pocket. Now several days after the surgery, Maxine was pleased with the way Luz was healing.

"Once you become more comfortable with the healing incision," Maxine said, "some women like to put vitamin E on the scar to lessen that 'I have a football stitch on my belly' look."

Luz smiled. "Thanks. I'll give that a try."

"You can sit up now," Maxine said. Luz was still fully dressed. Baggy sweats were the only apparel she could wear comfortably. Follow-up visits after successful surgery were some of Maxine's favorite moments at the office. Helping women had been a goal of hers for as long as she could remember.

"I'm actually getting a lot of mileage out of this at home," Luz said.

"Good." Maxine reached for a prescription pad and sat down on a stool beside her. "It's going to take you about six months to completely heal inside. I don't want you lifting anything heavy during that time." She finished scribbling the prescription and tore it off the pad. "Take one of these a day and come back to see me in a year if you have no other problems. A few weeks before your appointment, call my office for a referral for a mammogram. I want those results available when I see you the next time."

"That's it?" Luz asked as she adjusted her clothing.

"That's it." Maxine smiled. "One pill a day. The surgery put you into instant menopause."

Luz slowly slid off the examining table. "One pill a day. Hey, it's worth it."

It was a beautiful March morning and Maxine's turn to volunteer at the free clinic downtown. She arrived just as Blanche Marcaluso unlocked the front door to let in the staff and volunteers for the day. Maxine knew everyone who worked there since some of them volunteered their services on the same day every month that she did. Patients were already lined up outside the door, eager to be seen.

"Is someone bringing us breakfast?" one of the nurses asked as they filed into the reception area.

"Got it covered," Blanche said. "One drug rep is providing a Taco Cabana breakfast and another one is dropping off brisket plates for lunch."

"I hope it's not a bag full of bean and cheese tacos like the last time," the nurse said. She was short, in her late thirties, had dark curly hair and wore light blue scrubs. "I can't be seeing patients after a few of those."

"We'll save the potato and egg ones for you," Blanche said.

"Indeed," Maxine agreed. "These rooms are too small for the likes of that."

"I'll make a bean-and-cheese note for next time," Blanche said.

She passed out locks with a key attached for the lockers in the back so they could store their personal items. Maxine locked up her purse, but slipped her phone and pager in her white lab coat. The phone was turned off and her pager was on vibrate, but she liked having them both with her.

"The coffee's plugged in," Maxine heard someone up front say. "Get ready. Hook yourself up to the ass wagon and start the propeller! We're open for business!"

Maxine's first two patients were teenagers who were in the early stages of pregnancy and had decided to continue on in school. One would be giving her baby up for adoption, while the other wanted to keep hers. Maxine's third patient of the morning was a thirteen-year-old girl who was three months pregnant. She was there with her mother who looked to be in her mid twenties. They appeared to be more like siblings than mother and daughter.

Maxine had learned during her fourth year of medical school how not to be surprised by what she saw when it came to women's health issues and how pregnancies were faced by women of all ages. There were cultural issues to consider and there were moral issues to sort through when it came to reproduction rights. Maxine never judged a woman for the decisions she made. A woman's choice about whether or not to pursue motherhood was a very personal one. Maxine saw her job as one where she did her best to keep women healthy during the course of their reproductive years, as well as helping them see their way through menopause.

After the mother and daughter left, Blanche brought in a fresh cup of coffee for Maxine.

"You're a favorite around here," Blanche said.

"You tell that to all the free labor."

Blanche laughed. "Well, only to a point. With you, though, I actually mean it. The patients love you. Anyone who can make a thirteen-year-old feel at ease during a pelvic exam has my respect."

Maxine smiled. "Well, thanks. By the way, are there any tacos left? I misplaced the one I was working on earlier."

"A few bean and cheese," Blanche said. "I'm sure that's all there is in the bag by now. I'll bring you one before your next patient."

Maxine was always surprised at how much she enjoyed working at the clinic. The patient load was grueling and the pace much quicker than that of her own office, but the types of patients were a much different group than what she usually saw on a daily basis. Maxine's practice was geared toward the lesbian community and trendy upscale yuppie women who found it chic to have a female gynecologist. The time Maxine spent at the free clinic kept her in touch with all areas of her specialty and gave her a more diverse exposure to the local female population.

"One more patient," Blanche said as she popped her head in the room. "You holding up okay?"

Maxine laughed. "I'm fine." She pointed toward her foot. "Fresh sneakers. I'm good for another few hours or so."

The next patient was a young woman in her early twenties. She was five months pregnant and had been experiencing some spotting. Maxine glanced at the chart before going into the examining room. Blanche was in there already and would be serving as a chaperone.

"I'm Dr. Weston," Maxine said. "How are you feeling today, Ms. Stratford?"

"Fine," came the timid voice from the examination table.

She was draped in a long paper sheet; all Maxine could see of her was from the chin up.

"I understand you've had some spotting recently," Maxine said. "Scoot your bottom down toward the edge of the table, please. Has there been any cramping or pain?"

"No," the young woman replied.

Blanche helped the patient sit up and move where Maxine needed for her to be. By the time Blanche had her in the right position with feet in the stirrups, Maxine had latex gloves on and was sitting on the stool at the end of the exam table.

"Let's see what we've got here," Maxine said. "You'll feel some—"

She stopped for a moment and looked closer.

"What the . . ." Maxine mumbled with a frown. She raised up to look at the patient and couldn't see her face over the protruding swell of her stomach, so Maxine leaned to her left to get a side view of the woman's face.

"When was the last time you had intercourse?"

The woman giggled, then said meekly, "In the parking lot."

"The parking lot," Blanche repeated. "In *our* parking lot?"

"Hand me some tissues, please," Maxine said quietly.

"For the love of Peter," Blanche whispered as she gave her the box of tissues sitting on the counter.

"That about sums it up," Maxine said.

Chapter Seven

Maxine pulled into the driveway and was relieved to see that she had at least arrived before some of their guests. Blanche and Phoebe's truck was parked in front of the house, but Elaine and Cheryl weren't there yet. Maxine grabbed the two bottles of wine and a fresh loaf of French bread and got out of her car. If she was lucky, there wouldn't be a patient requiring Dr. Weston's attention for the evening.

"Ah!" Betina said when Maxine came into the kitchen from the garage entrance. "The wine is here. I can't believe I forgot to get this yesterday."

Maxine set the wine bottles and bread on the counter before hugging her lover and greeting their two guests. As she fumbled with getting the cork out of the first bottle of wine, the doorbell rang.

"That should be Elaine and Cheryl," Betina announced. "Will you get that, darlin'?"

Maxine took the wine bottle with her to the front door. "Come in! Come in!" She gave them both hugs and motioned toward the kitchen. "Whatever that is you're carrying, it certainly smells good."

"Swedish meatballs," Cheryl said. "They're still warm."

"The car smelled fabulous on the way over," Elaine said.

"Is that my daughter-the-doctor?" Blanche asked from the dining room. She poked her head around the corner and laughed.

"Yes, it is!" Elaine said.

"I have you on the schedule for Wednesday. That's still good, right?"

"Yes, Mom," Elaine said. "I'm all yours on Wednesday." She gave her mother a hug.

"How's the skin business, Doc?" Phoebe asked. It was her standard way of greeting her lover's dermatologist daughter.

"I've had a rash of patients recently," Elaine said as she gave Phoebe a hug. "Some a bit flakier than others. How are you?"

"I'll be better once I sample one of those meatballs. Oh, I heard a rumor today. Something about walking backward on a treadmill reverses age. True or false?"

Elaine threw her head back and laughed. "False, I'm afraid."

"Speaking of flaky patients," Blanche said. "Maxine had a doozy yesterday. You're still coming back, aren't you?" she asked her. "That one didn't burn you out on the clinic, did she? Please, say no. Please?"

"Why?" Elaine asked. "What happened?"

Maxine got more glasses out of the china cabinet and began to pour their guests some wine. She just smiled and shook her head as she passed the drinks around.

"Her last patient of the day," Blanche said. "Five months pregnant, up on the table, nervous like they all are in the stirrups. Maxine begins the examination and then casually asked the woman when was the last time she had intercourse. When the patient said 'in the parking lot,' I thought I would die."

"The parking lot?" Phoebe said with comically wide eyes. "She had sex just before her OB exam?"

"That's right!"

Maxine continued shaking her head and speared a meatball with a toothpick.

"My goodness," Cheryl said with a curled up nose. "What did you say to her?"

"Not much," Maxine replied. "I'm no longer surprised by what I find during an examination anymore. Old forgotten tampons, remnants of a cucumber, Rolos, candle wax. Lots of things get left up there."

"Rolos?" Phoebe said. "Rolos the candy?"

"Actually, Rolos and a cherry Life Saver once. Different women, though."

"My goodness," Cheryl said again.

"All I know is, I was in shock for a few seconds there," Blanche said. "The thought of someone having sex in our little clinic parking lot sort of freaked me out." She scooped up a few meatballs from the casserole dish and put them on a small plate. "But you were cool, Maxine. I'll give you that. You were cool!"

"What did the patient have to say for herself?" Phoebe grumbled. "As a nurse, I've seen a lot of dumb things in my day. I would've told her a thing or two."

"She had a nervous giggle," Maxine said. "I'm sure she was embarrassed."

"Oh!" Blanche said after chewing on her first meatball. "I remember this now! Maxine asked for some tissues to tidy up the area a little—"

"Ewww!"

"And I heard her say under her breath, 'That's like eating Oreos before going to the dentist'," Blanche said before she howled with laughter. That set the others off into peals of their own.

"Well, not really," Maxine said. "I was being kind. The Oreo and dentist analogy didn't involve a penis in the parking lot."

As the level of laughter increased once again, Maxine looked up and saw Betina standing in the doorway of the kitchen with a blank expression on her face. She seemed confused and oblivious to what was going on in the dining room. Maxine piled a few more meatballs on a clean plate and took them over to her.

"As long as that sex-in-the-parking-lot incident didn't burn you out on volunteering at the clinic," Blanche said, "then I'll just consider it another episode of bad judgment on the part of a patient. We need you there."

"No, I'm fine," Maxine said. "It comes with the territory. I would spend more time there if I could."

"Rolos?" Phoebe said again. "Why would Rolos be stuck up there?"

"You okay, baby?" Maxine asked as she popped a meatball into Betina's mouth.

"I can't believe I forgot to buy the wine."

"It's taken care of," Maxine said. "We have plenty now. This isn't a drinking crowd anyway."

"Need help with anything?" Cheryl asked.

Maxine was relieved to have Cheryl's help in getting things moving in the right direction. The three of them worked on a cheese and fruit tray and got it ready to serve.

"Even though it's still too cool to swim," Maxine said to everyone, "it should be nice out by the pool."

"Who thinks the mayor's smoking ban will pass if it's on the ballot in the fall?" Phoebe asked awhile later.

They all had plates piled up with sandwiches, pickles, olives, chips, fruit, cheese, and meatballs. Cheryl and Elaine were sitting at the edge of the pool with their bare feet dangling in the water, while the others were not far away in chaises on the patio.

"That's a tough one," Cheryl said. "The rights of business owners to voice what they want their businesses to be like, verses the rights of a nonsmoker who would prefer a smoke-free environment to dine in has been pretty much argued to death lately. I think the vote could go either way. Some think the government has too much power over us already."

"I agree," Blanche said. "It's not even an 'us the nonsmokers' verses 'them the smokers' issue any longer."

"It's coming down to whether or not we want the government dictating and legislating what we do every day," Cheryl added. "Even though I'm a nonsmoker, I'm inclined to vote against the ban."

"I had a patient tell me once that quitting smoking was easy," Phoebe said. "He'd done it twenty or thirty times already."

Maxine glanced over at Betina sitting beside her in a chaise and noticed her picking at her food.

"Want me to get you something else?" Maxine asked.

"No," Betina said. "I must've snacked too much. I'm not hungry."

"Do we have dessert?" someone asked.

Betina smiled. "Apple pie and vanilla ice cream."

"I think my daughter-the-lawyer and her girlfriend are on the outs again," Blanche announced, referring to her other gay daughter, Mickey Marcaluso. "I don't get it. We're in the age where sex can kill you. Why can't lesbians just try and work things out?"

"For some women, the true measure of desire is in the pursuit," Phoebe said. "They've got no stickability these days. They get a thrill from all the flirting and the other highs of being with someone new, then once they catch 'em, the fun's over. Time to move on."

"Ooohhh!" Elaine said. "Listen to you! Being all profound over there. 'The true measure of desire is in the pursuit.' That's bumper sticker material if I ever heard it."

"I think I read that on a bathroom door at the airport earlier this week," Phoebe said.

"Well, it's certainly the way some young people think these days."

"Stickability," Cheryl said. "I like that word. It's very descriptive and says exactly what's lacking in younger people these days. It's not just lesbians, you know. It's everyone. When times get tough, they move on. They don't try and fix anything. It's easier to just start over with someone new."

"It's what I like to call the Bullshit Factor," Blanche said. "To me, it's all bullshit, but sometimes you just need *fresh* bullshit. I've done it with jobs and I've seen others do it with women. They leave the old bullshit behind and go looking for fresh bullshit somewhere else."

"Just don't be getting any ideas there," Phoebe said.

Blanche laughed. "Nah. I happen to like your bullshit."

Maxine reached over and took Betina's hand. At that moment she felt very lucky.

Twenty minutes later as Phoebe stretched out on the chaise, she announced, "I'm so full I could pop." The moon poked through some clouds, while soft music from the stereo drifted out onto the patio. It was so nice and peaceful that Maxine's eyes were getting heavy.

"I'm full, too," Blanche said. "Any more of that pie left?"

Their laughter had become more subdued and all six of them were now in chaises lost in their own thoughts. Maxine felt mellow even though she wasn't drinking. She would sleep well after their guests went home.

"I love being a lesbian," Phoebe said. "I wouldn't change it for anything."

"Neither would I," Elaine agreed.

"In fact," Phoebe said, "when I die, just cremate me, put me in a douche bottle and run me through one more time."

"Oh, good Lord!"

"I'm serious!"

"No more wine for you," Blanche said.

After the laughter died down, Betina said, "I had a client today tell me that she drinks some of her urine every day for medicinal purposes."

"Ewww!"

"That's probably a lot more common than people realize," Cheryl said. "Some Indian tribes do it religiously. There are also some monks who indulge in that practice."

"How old was this client?" Phoebe asked.

"About your age," Betina said. "Nice lady. Great hair. Good tipper."

"You mean old like me?" Phoebe said with a laugh.

"You're not old yet," Betina said.

"The older the violin, the sweeter the music," Blanche said as she reached for Phoebe's hand.

"We're all a bunch of walking bumper stickers tonight," Elaine commented.

"That reminds me," Phoebe said. "I need a haircut. Can you work me in next week?"

"Call me tomorrow at the shop and I'll let you know what's available," Betina said. "If I have to, I'll stay late one day to do you."

The "do you" remark sent another chuckle around the semicircle before they all got quiet again. Maxine could hear crickets chirping in the yard and an Eagles song drifting out onto the patio.

"So what's the answer?" Betina asked sleepily. "Is drinking your own urine good for you?"

"I personally wouldn't recommend it," Blanche said. "Can't make your breath smell that good either."

"My brother Joey overheard the conversation," Betina said. "He was giving a perm right next to us and had an interesting idea." She stretched out on the chaise and got more comfortable before reaching for Maxine's hand again. "After the woman admitted to drinking her own urine, Joey suggested she freeze it and make pissicles."

"Ha!" Phoebe blurted out before the others began to laugh. "I think I've heard it all now!"

"Can't see that one on a bumper sticker."

"Pissicles," Maxine said with a chuckle. She squeezed Betina's hand and continued enjoying the company of their friends.

Maxine turned out all the lights in the house and locked the doors. It had been such a fun, relaxing evening that Maxine wondered why they didn't have their friends over more often. She left the living room drapes open and could see Mr. Gardner across the street with his binoculars focused on her. With his kitchen light on in the room behind him, she could see into his house just as well as he could probably see into hers. She resisted the urge to wave at him and decided to close the drapes instead. Maxine imagined him grumbling on his way to bed, feeling disappointed at not having a little show to wrap up his evening.

She found her way to the bedroom in the dark and brushed her teeth in the bathroom. She wasn't surprised to see Betina asleep already since she had been tired most of the evening. Maxine slipped into bed after a quick shower and reached for Betina under the covers. Warm and sweet-smelling, Betina made a little cooing noise to acknowledge Maxine's presence, but didn't give any indication that she wanted anything other than to be cuddled.

"Goodnight, baby," Maxine whispered before kissing Betina's bare back. She too drifted off to sleep without another thought.

Chapter Eight

Even though it was Saturday morning, Maxine was still on call. She woke up at six-thirty to her answering service relaying a message from a patient. The Garza baby was three weeks early and on its way.

She got out of bed and took another quick shower to wake up. Maxine dressed in khaki slacks and a yellow V-neck T-shirt. She went to the closet to get one of her pre-packed gym bags with clean scrubs and another change of clothes in it, but she didn't see any of the bags in their usual place.

Hmm, she thought. Betina always had at least two gym bags ready for her to use. Maxine glanced around the bedroom and saw three of the bags in the corner by the recliner. She opened up each one and discovered they all contained the dirty scrubs she had brought home during the week.

What the hell? she thought, but Maxine didn't really have time to worry about it. She could change into hospital scrubs once she got there. *I have another set of clothes at the office if I need them for some reason*, she thought.

Maxine went over to the bed and gave Betina a kiss and covered her up with the sheet and bedspread.

"I'm off to the hospital," she whispered. "I'll call you later."

"Give your baby a kiss," Betina said sleepily. She still had her eyes closed.

Maxine smiled and gave her another one. After a peck on the cheek, she said, "I'll call you once I'm on my way home later."

"What are you doing here on a Saturday, Dr. Marcaluso?" Maxine asked Elaine as they stood in front of the main bank of elevators at the hospital.

"I have a young patient with an infected tattoo," Elaine said. "His parents are furious."

"Infected bad enough to be hospitalized? I don't blame them."

"It's amazing what you can get at a flea market these days," Elaine said. "Tattoos. Piercings. Infections."

They got on the elevator and took the short ride up, then followed the small crowd to the cafeteria. Maxine appeared to be the more casual of the two with her green hospital scrubs, sneakers and a white lab coat. Elaine, on the other hand, presented a more professional flair for fashion in a dark blue skirt, powder blue cotton blouse and a white lab coat.

"We had fun last night," Elaine said. "We should get together like that more often."

"I agree. I had fun, too." Maxine selected a ham and cheese sandwich and a small container of orange juice off the grab-n-go cart.

"An emergency or the usual today?" Elaine asked her. She paid for a small salad and a tuna sandwich.

"A five-pound-three-ounce girl with a full head of coal-black hair. She'll be a looker like her mother in another sixteen years or so."

"What are you two doing tomorrow?" Elaine asked as she nudged Maxine toward an empty table.

"A quiet day at home together would be a nice change," Maxine said. "I also need to work on a paper."

"Mom and Phoebe want to see a Spurs game next week. I can pick up six tickets if you two are interested."

Maxine laughed. "Each time we've gone to a game, all Betina does is complain about the bad dye-jobs the Silver Dancers have."

"Then there's something for all of us at the games," Elaine said with a chuckle. "That's the only time Cheryl will touch a hot dog."

"I'll ask the little woman about it and get back with you."

Elaine grinned. "How much trouble would you be in if Betina knew you called her that?"

"None, probably. But just in case, how about we don't mention it to her?"

"When are you scheduled to work at the clinic again?" Elaine asked. "Maybe we can do it together soon."

"I usually shoot for the second Tuesday and fourth Thursday of the month," Maxine said. "And a half day here and there if my office schedule is light enough." Her pager went off. Maxine unhooked it from the waistband of her scrubs. "That better be the little woman now," she said as she looked at the phone number on the small digital display. "But no such luck."

Maxine pulled her cell phone out of her lab coat pocket and took another swig of orange juice as she pushed a button on the phone.

"Yes, Woody," she said. "What can I do for you?"

"Where are you?"

"In the hospital cafeteria eating breakfast." She glanced at the clock on the wall over the cashier's head. "Make that lunch. I'm eating lunch."

"Oh! Oh! That's beautiful! I'm scrubbing in for a delivery now and I've got another patient on her way in. She's in her first trimester and experiencing heavy bleeding. Can you meet her in the ER for me?"

"What's the patient's name?"

❧

61

Maxine was tired when she got home later that afternoon. As soon as she walked into the kitchen from the garage entrance, she noticed the sink was still full of dirty dishes from the party the night before. An overflowing trash bag propped up against the door to the pantry also caught her attention. When Maxine went into the living room, she found Betina asleep on the sofa with the television on. She went over to the sofa and sat on the edge. Betina stretched and slowly opened her eyes.

"How long have you been home?" Maxine asked. She had called Betina as soon as she left the hospital about twenty minutes earlier, but had gotten the answering machine.

"A few hours," Betina said. "Joey took my late appointments today."

"Are you feeling all right?"

"I'm fine. Just tired."

"Yeah, so am I."

Maxine got up and went into the bedroom. She saw the three gym bags right where she had left them, with the dirty clothes still inside each one. Maxine also noticed that the bed hadn't been made that day. Suddenly, the messy state of her surroundings was even more noticeable as she scanned the room. She emptied the three gym bags on the bed and then gathered up all the dirty clothes. Maxine took them to the hamper in the bathroom and found it too full to hold anything else.

"I need to do some laundry," Betina said as she sat down on the side of the bed.

Maxine put the pile of dirty clothes she was holding on top of the hamper. The closer she looked, the more cluttered the bedroom appeared to be. There were several pairs of shoes sticking out from under the bed and a pile of magazines on Betina's nightstand.

What the hell is going on here? Maxine wondered. *This place has never looked this cluttered and messy.*

She went to her dresser and took out three old sets of scrubs and enough clean underwear and socks for each gym bag. She liked having a fresh set of clothes with her at all times for various things that came up during the course of the day, but couldn't find three clean pairs of slacks to accomplish that particular goal at the moment.

"Did you pick up any dry cleaning this week?" Maxine asked.

"No," Betina said with a sigh. "I forgot all about it." She got up and left the bedroom.

Maxine went to her closet to see what was in there. She wasn't used to fending for herself this way and it irked her to have to do it now. She packed up the three spare gym bags and remembered there was another one in her car with more dirty clothes in it. On her way to the garage to retrieve it, Maxine once again saw the dirty dishes in the sink and the overflowing trash by the pantry. She heard a noise on the patio and glanced out the kitchen window into the back yard. Betina was sitting in a chaise by the pool. *Hmm. I thought she was going to do some laundry!*

Maxine went outside into the back yard where Betina seemed to already be asleep again.

"Hey," Maxine called. "Are you *sure* you're feeling okay?"

"I told you I was tired."

Maxine nodded. "Yes, you mentioned that."

"A boy or a girl today?"

Maxine smiled. "A girl. She had so much hair she looked like a little hedgehog." She sat on one of the chaises next to Betina's. "What's the matter, baby? This isn't like you."

"I don't know. I keep thinking if I just get a good night's sleep I'll feel better."

"We were in bed sort of early last night. What time did you get up this morning?"

"Joey called at about ten. I missed an appointment with my first client. I was able to get there for the next one, though."

This really isn't like her, Maxine thought. She leaned over and gave her a light kiss on the lips. "We'll go to bed early tonight, okay?" Maxine stood up and straightened her shirt. "What sounds good for dinner? The sandwich I had for lunch wore off hours ago."

"Something easy," Betina said.

"You want to go out?"

"No."

"How about a pizza?" Maxine suggested.

"Yes," Betina said. "Good idea."

Maxine's cell phone rang. It was her partner, Woody. She walked back into the house to talk to him.

"So how is she?" Maxine asked.

"Got the bleeding stopped," Woody said. Maxine could tell he was on his cell phone in his car. "Thanks for being there."

"No problem," she said. "That fate thing was working today. See you on Monday if not sooner."

Maxine put her cell phone away and went back to the kitchen to bag up the trash. She opened up the dishwasher and saw it was full of dirty dishes.

"Grrr."

She put dishwashing detergent in the dishwasher and started up that load. Remembering the other gym bag in her car, Maxine went out into the garage to retrieve it. As she made her way back to the bedroom, she could feel herself getting even more agitated by the little things that were now coming to her attention: an empty coffee cup with a bright red lipstick print sitting on top of the magazines, toothpaste globs on the bathroom vanity, a pile of towels behind the bathroom door. Where was the order she was accustomed to? When did such sloppiness take over their lives? Why hadn't she noticed any of this before?

Maxine placed the soiled towels on top of the hamper with the other dirty clothes she had put there earlier. She dragged the hamper through the house and into the laundry room off the side of the kitchen. As she passed by the kitchen sink once more, Maxine again noticed the dirty dishes piled up. She looked out the kitchen window to find Betina still asleep in the chaise.

"Hmm," Maxine said to herself. "That's not happening." She went back through the living room and opened the sliding glass door that led to the patio. She gave Betina's shoulder a little shake. "Hey, wake up. Are you okay?"

Betina opened her eyes and stretched. "Is the pizza here?"

"Not yet. Come on, babe. Get up or you won't sleep later." She offered a hand to help pull her up from the chaise. "I thought you were going to do some laundry?"

"I was, but this is as far as I got." Betina slipped her arms around Maxine's waist and laid her head on her shoulder. "Hold me."

Maxine's irritation melted away as she took Betina into her arms. *How can you stay mad at this beautiful, sexy woman?* she thought.

Maxine washed the dishes in the sink while Betina sorted the dirty laundry and got a load of wash started.

"When's that pizza getting here?" Maxine asked. "I'm hungry."

"I don't know," Betina said. "What time did you call it in?"

Maxine stopped rinsing a plate and turned to look at her. "What time did *I* call it in?"

"Yes," Betina said. "What time did *you* call it in? You were the one with a phone in your hand."

"That was a business call. Who did you think was on the phone? The pizza boy asking what kind of pizza we wanted?" Maxine set the soapy plate down in the sink. "In the five years we've been together and the hundreds of pizzas we've consumed at home over the years, how many of them have I ever ordered?"

"Tell me where it says I'm the only person in this house who's allowed to order a pizza?" Betina shot back.

Maxine couldn't believe they were having this conversation, and she was surprised at how quickly Betina had lost her temper.

"*You* were the one with the phone when we talked about ordering a pizza," Betina noted. "Was there a phone out there on the patio with me? Nooo! Are you incapable of ordering a pizza? Nooo! You order tests for patients all day long! Getting a pizza shouldn't be that hard!"

Maxine dried her hands off on the bottom of her blouse and whipped out her cell phone. "What's the number?"

"Look it up!" Betina snapped. She marched over to the refrigerator and peeled off a Pizza Hut magnet and handed it to her. "There you go. Knock yourself out."

"Thank you," Maxine said and snatched the magnet from her.

They still weren't speaking by the time the pizza finally arrived. Maxine took a few slices to her study and worked on some revisions to a paper she hoped to have published. After about an hour, she was ready for another slice of pizza and something else to drink. Ordinarily Betina would have been in there checking to see if she needed anything. Maxine decided to take a break and see what Betina was doing. She found her asleep on the sofa with the TV on and a half-eaten pizza slice on a plate setting on the coffee table. Maxine eased down on the edge of the sofa and woke her up.

"Why don't you go to bed, baby?"

Betina opened her eyes and let out a long sigh. "Will you come with me?"

"Soon. I have some more work to do first."

Betina put her arms around Maxine's neck and pulled her down for a kiss.

Tired of being snippy and already missing their usual pizza-night routine where they usually both fell asleep on the sofa, Maxine said, "I'm sorry about what happened earlier."

"Me, too." She kissed the side of Maxine's neck. "I like being in a household where both people know how to order a pizza."

Maxine chuckled. "What does that mean?"

"I think sometimes you forget that I work, too. You're not the only one with a full-time job."

Maxine pulled away to get a better look at her.

"I'm in business with my brother just like you're in business with Woody," Betina said. "I have a lot of responsibility outside of this house, too."

"I know you do."

"Really?" Betina asked. "Do you?" She touched a perfectly manicured finger to the tip of Maxine's nose. "I'm on my feet all day long, too. The women you operate on are at least asleep when you're working on them. Mine are awake and usually bitchy."

"It's not my fault your clients aren't getting anesthesia before you give them highlights and a perm," Maxine said lightly.

Betina took her finger away. "Far be it from me to have a bad day at work and expect a little pampering when I get home."

Momentarily confused by the sharp tone of Betina's voice, Maxine asked her what happened at work that day.

"That's hardly the point."

"Then what *is* the point?"

They looked at each other again, but neither said anything for a moment. Finally, Maxine said, "Tell me what's wrong."

"I don't know."

"Why are you angry with me?"

"It's not you."

"Then what is it? Talk to me."

"I don't know."

"Well, something's going on with you."

"I'm just tired."

Maxine looked at her closely again and then nodded. "Okay."

They stared at each other for another long moment before Betina said, "Okay what?"

Maxine shrugged. "Just okay. I don't know what else to say." Finding herself at a total loss for words, she gave her an impulsive hug. "Why don't you go to bed? I'll be along later."

Feeling as though she had missed something important or forgotten a birthday or anniversary, Maxine mentally clicked off the dates that were significant to them, but nothing came to her. She got up and went back to her study to do more work on her paper. Whatever was going on with Betina, Maxine hoped everything would resolve itself soon.

Chapter Nine

Maxine got to her office early and put the finishing touches on her manuscript. She left a note by the coffee pot in the break area, playing into the running office joke about letting her staff know when she was in the office. Over a year ago Maxine had walked in on an employee discussion about what a good boss and doctor she was. Her sudden appearance in the break room seemed to embarrass everyone. She was promptly scolded about being in the office without anyone's knowledge, so Maxine now made it a point to keep her staff informed of her exact whereabouts whenever she was anywhere in the area.

By mid-morning, she and her receptionist had faxed the manuscript back and forth to the publisher three times before revisions were agreed upon by both parties. In addition to having to revise the paper, Maxine not only had her own block of patients to tend to for the day, but her partner, Dr. Woodrow Clarkson, was called away for a delivery, leaving Maxine with even more patients than originally scheduled. At the end of a long afternoon, she was tired and cranky. The one time Betina had called her, Maxine had been unavailable to talk.

She pulled into the garage at home and went in the side door to the kitchen. Fresh dirty dishes were in the sink and the dishwasher was open, sporting clean dishes that hadn't been put away yet. The bag of trash Maxine had taken care of the day before was still sitting where she had left it by the pantry.

"I thought I heard you come in," Betina said from the doorway to the dining room. "How was your day?"

"Busy," Maxine said. "I'm sorry I missed your call earlier."

"Mona said it was a zoo there."

"What's for dinner?" Maxine asked. She was hungry and couldn't even remember having lunch.

"Could've been leftover pizza, but you forgot to put it away last night."

"Me?" Maxine said with a furrowed brow. "*I* forgot to put it away?"

"Who was the last one awake? I went to bed early, remember?"

Since Betina was always the one who tidied up and put things away, Maxine was surprised by the comment.

"So we can either have cold cuts that were left from the party last week or we can go out."

"Let's go out," Maxine said. "I want real food."

"Then let me take a quick shower and I'll be ready."

Maxine went into the living room and turned on the TV to watch the news. She didn't want to go out. She wanted a quiet evening at home with something good and tasty cooking in the oven. Stretching out on the sofa, she attempted to surf all ninety-nine channels, but apparently the cable wasn't working and only local stations were available. Nothing held her attention anyway. A while later Betina breezed in from the bedroom with her hair wet, smelling like spring. Dressed in white shorts, sandals, and a pink cotton blouse, she was stunning even though her hair wasn't even combed yet. Betina was one of those women who could look good in anything. She tanned easily, and with the metabolism of a butterfly, she ate what she wanted, never gaining weight and keeping her curves in all the right places.

At first, when they had started going out more and attended a monthly lesbian social gathering called First Wednesday Night, not many of the women associated with the organization seemed to warm up to Betina. Maxine overheard one woman comment that Betina "looked too straight" to be a lesbian. There might have been a compliment in there somewhere, but Maxine didn't care to have strangers discussing her lover in such a way as if "looking too straight"—whatever *that* meant—was a bad thing.

There were several beautiful and interesting women who attended the First Wednesday Night events, representing a large array of professions and businesses in the lesbian community. It provided a good, safe forum to network and meet new people. Many of the women were patients of Maxine's already and once it was known that Betina was her lover, she, too, had been able to get new clients from the First Wednesday Night group. But it had been Maxine's experience that initially most women were intimidated by Betina's confidence and her classically blond good looks. It wasn't until someone took the time to get to know the warm, generous person inside that Betina began to seem more real to them.

"You ready?" Betina asked as she ran her fingers through the back of her hair.

"Yes," Maxine said. She glanced at her curiously from the sofa. "Are you?"

"I'm ready. Let's go."

Hmm, Maxine thought. *She's actually going to leave the house without putting on any makeup?* There had been times when Maxine saw Betina sketch on eyeliner and lipstick before even opening the front door to get the Sunday paper out of the yard. *Maybe she's hungry and plans on "foo-fooing up" once we're in the car,* she thought.

"What sounds good for dinner?" Maxine asked a few minutes later as she backed out of the driveway.

"I don't care. You decide."

"I'm in the mood for Chinese. How does that sound?"

"Anything but Chinese."

"Okay," Maxine said. "Mexican food?"

"I had that for lunch."

"Seafood?"

"I don't care. You decide."

Maxine shook her head and drove to the nearest seafood restaurant. Occasionally she glanced to her right to see what Betina was doing. Her irritation softened when Betina reached for her hand and gave it a pat.

Maxine took the menu the waitress gave her and perused the specials. After placing their orders, she studied Betina more closely for a moment.

"Are you mad at me about something?" Maxine asked.

Betina took her time squeezing a lemon wedge into her ice tea. "Should I be?"

"No."

Betina smiled. Her hair had dried already and looked just as good with next to no attention as most people's did after having it done professionally. Maxine wanted to get this discussion out of the way before their meal arrived. There were too many weird things happening lately. Something was going on, but she didn't yet have a clear grasp of what it was. Occasionally Betina liked to string her along when something displeased her.

"Does this have anything to do with the pizza being left out last night?" Maxine asked.

Betina dropped the lemon wedge into her glass. "I would hope not. How petty do you think I am?"

"Please don't make me keep guessing. You know how I hate that."

71

"Since when have I ever been able to make you do anything?"

"Since day one?"

They laughed together and Betina nodded. "Well . . . yeah."

Maxine fixed her napkin and lined up her silverware on the table. "So you're not upset with me about something?" she asked again after a moment. When Betina didn't answer, Maxine said, "Just tell me what it is or what I did. Give me a place to start. Are you not feeling appreciated enough? Am I being an asshole and not realizing it?"

The waitress brought their salads and to Maxine's surprise, she saw tears in Betina's eyes.

"Baby, what's the matter? Talk to me."

Betina shook her head. "I don't know."

"You have to know something. Talk to me. Is it Joey? Is it work? Is it something I'm not doing or something I'm doing and not *supposed* to do? What is it?"

Betina poked at her salad and cut up a cherry tomato. "I'll let you know when I figure it out."

Oh, great, Maxine thought. She knew then that it would be best to just drop the subject, but she wanted at least a small clue about why Betina was so tired all the time and why there had been so many changes in their usual routine lately.

"Maybe we should check into getting someone to come in and clean a few times a week," Maxine suggested. Betina didn't comment. She kept nudging at the lettuce on her plate. "I think Phoebe and Blanche have someone they use."

"Do you really want a stranger in our home?"

Maxine shrugged. "You were right about us both being busy. Your client base is larger now than it's ever been and it's obvious I'm not much help when it comes to domestic issues."

"Domestic issues?" Betina said, rolling her eyes. "You can't even stick leftover pizza in the fridge."

Sensing a break in Betina's melancholy mood, Maxine gladly continued and even enjoyed having Betina point out a few of her shortcomings.

"Ahh! So this *is* about me leaving the pizza out!"

With a slight smirk, Betina asked, "What exactly do you think about when you're closing up the house before going to bed?"

Maxine shrugged. "I think about what I have to do the next day. Will I be in surgery all morning? Or will I be in the clinic?" She opened up a small package of crackers. "Why? What do you think about before you get ready for bed?"

As if the answer were very simple, Betina looked at her and said, "If I'm the last one up, I think about whether or not there's any pizza that needs to go in the fridge."

When they returned home after dinner, Maxine sat on the sofa and switched on the TV. The cable was out, so she left it on a local channel and picked up an obstetrics and gynecology periodical from a stack on the coffee table. She had another paper to work on and glanced at her watch to see how late it was. Betina came into the living room and sat down beside her. She handed Maxine a cold bottle of water and put her head on Maxine's shoulder.

"Thought any more about getting a housekeeper?" Maxine asked.

"A little," she said quietly, "but you know me. I'm the kind of person who would have to clean up the house before the house-keeper came over to clean up the house."

Maxine kissed the top of her head. "Why don't I give Blanche a call and see who they use and how much picking up they feel comfortable doing beforehand?"

"I'm sorry I can't keep up with everything."

Maxine rubbed her cheek against Betina's hair. "I wish you had mentioned something sooner."

"It snuck up on me," Betina said sleepily. "There's just so much to do."

"All I know is, I'll never look at a pizza box the same again."

⁂

The next day at the office, Maxine gave Blanche Marcaluso a call. "You're not canceling on Wednesday, are you?" Blanche asked.

"No," Maxine said. "Not at all." She moved her rolodex back to its original place on her desk. "I need your help with something." She went on to explain how she and Betina were in need of a house-keeper.

"We use a woman by the name of Ann Kingston," Blanche said. "She's in great demand, too. I'm not sure she could work you in."

"Oh," Maxine said, disappointed.

"I could give her a call for you, or give her your number. She's about my age and has a helper, but they do excellent work and come with a long list of references."

"A reference from you is good enough for me. What's her number? I'll call her."

Maxine placed a call to a pager and left her office number. A few hours later she and Ann Kingston finally connected. Ann explained that she had an opening in her schedule and could fit them in twice a month on every other Thursday. She wanted to see the house first and get a sense of what they needed.

"Unless there's an emergency," Maxine said, "Betina and I can be home tomorrow afternoon if that's okay."

They fine-tuned arrangements to meet the next day and Maxine gave her the address.

"We've got one in the chute," Mona said after she knocked on Maxine's office door and then stuck her head in.

Maxine nodded and said into the phone, "We'll see you tomorrow afternoon then." She hung up and went out into the hallway. There was a chart in the clear plastic holder outside of examining room two. As Maxine headed in that direction, she heard a commotion in one of the offices that faced the reception area.

"Someone just fainted in the waiting room," Mona said.

Maxine followed her through the maze of passageways to the door that led to the waiting area. Maxine found her nurse Sandy and a pregnant patient kneeling on the floor over an unconscious young woman. Other patients had closed their magazines and were whispering to each other.

"Is she breathing?" Maxine asked as she knelt down beside them.

"Yes," Alberta said. "She's got a strong pulse."

"What's the nature of her appointment today?"

"She's one of Dr. Clarkson's patients," Sandy said, "but didn't have an appointment. She mentioned being into day five of heavy bleeding."

Mona arrived with a first aid kit and a wheelchair. Maxine found a small ammonia ampoule and popped it open to wave under the young woman's nose. A few seconds later she started to cough and come around. Maxine helped her sit up, then she and Mona got her into the wheelchair. Sandy wheeled the patient back where they could take her blood pressure and make her more comfortable.

"I'll check her chart for an emergency number in case we need it," Mona said.

Maxine turned around and addressed the other wide-eyed patients in the waiting room. "Everyone feel okay? If not, let us know now while we have this nice little first aid kit here."

One of the women said, "I haven't been able to see my feet in a month. Got anything in there that'll help?"

By the end of the day, Maxine was tired from the constant flow of patients as well as having to perform an emergency procedure. There was a lot of bleeding when Maxine examined the woman who had fainted. She ruined a pair of blue slacks during the exam. Maxine changed clothes and stuffed the stained ones in a gym bag for disposal later. By the time she got home, all she wanted to do was unwind, have a nice dinner and go to bed early. She was scheduled to be in surgery the next morning.

Chapter Ten

Maxine pulled into the driveway and tried to use her garage door opener, but it wouldn't work. After thumping the remote a few times with no results, she parked the car and turned off the engine. Before she could gather her things and open the car door, Betina pulled in behind her.

Maxine got out and went to ask her to open the garage door, but when she reached Betina's car, she found her sitting there gripping the steering wheel, looking straight ahead. Maxine knocked on the window to get her attention and then made a "roll down your window" motion with her hand. When Betina didn't acknowledge her, Maxine knocked again. Finally, Betina rolled down the window about a third of the way.

"Are you okay?" Maxine asked, but didn't get an answer. "Betina? What's the matter?"

"I couldn't get the garage door to open," Betina said in a small, subdued voice.

"Oh," Maxine said. "Well, crap. Neither can I. The thing was fine this morning. I thought my batteries in the remote were old."

"That's not it," Betina said, then she started to cry. "I don't know how this happened."

Maxine was shocked to see the tears. "Baby, what's the matter?" She tried to open the door, but it was locked. Hurrying around to the other side of the car, she got into the passenger's seat. The air conditioner was blowing full blast and Betina continued gripping the steering wheel and looking straight ahead. "Come here," Maxine said. "What in the world is wrong?"

"I don't know how this happened," Betina said again just before she began to sob.

A jolt of icy fear ran through Maxine's veins. "My goodness! What's the matter, baby? Tell me what happened," Maxine said as she opened her arms and pulled Betina toward her. "Why are you so upset?"

"The electricity," Betina said in between sobs. "They turned it off."

"They? They who?" *What the hell is going on here?* she thought.

"The power company."

"Whose electricity?"

"*Our* electricity!"

"What?" Maxine said as she continued to hold her. She managed to turn and look at the house, but there was still enough daylight outside to make everything appear normal. "How could that happen? Why would they do such a thing?"

Betina began sobbing even harder then.

"It's okay," Maxine said soothingly as she kissed the top of her lover's head. "Please don't do this, baby."

Having Betina so distraught made Maxine cry as well. She had never seen her this upset before. "It's okay. Please don't cry." She gave her a long hug and kissed the side of her face. "Tell me what happened."

Betina sniffed and let out a heavy sigh as she dried her eyes on the sleeve of her blouse. She had black smudges where her mascara had run. In a halting, broken voice she began to explain.

"I came home . . . about . . . an hour . . . ago," Betina said. She sat up in her seat and looked to the left, away from Maxine. "The garage door wouldn't open, so . . . I had to go in through the . . . front door." She took several quick gulping breaths before continuing. "When I got . . . to the porch, I saw a . . . a piece of paper stuck on the door." She broke down again, and Maxine waited a moment for her to get control of herself. "It's there . . . in the backseat somewhere."

Maxine leaned over the seat and found a wadded-up piece of paper. She unfolded it and smoothed it out enough to read: Notice of Service Termination Due to Lack of Payment.

The flyer was from City Public Service and had a phone number to call to reestablish service.

Momentarily confused by what she read, Maxine said, "Terminated due to lack of payment? How could that happen?"

Betina put her hands over her face and began to sob again. The sound was heart-wrenching and made Maxine's eyes immediately fill with tears once more.

"Let's go inside, baby," Maxine whispered.

"I can't," she said through her fingers and tears. "It's too . . . depressing and it's . . . too damn . . . hot in there."

Maxine took out her cell phone and dialed the emergency number on the crumpled flyer.

"I already . . . did that," Betina said with a sniff. "Can't get it turned back on . . . until tomorrow morning . . . at the earliest."

"Tomorrow?"

Betina nodded as fresh tears rolled down her already wet face.

"I still don't understand how this happened."

Another small sob escaped from Betina's throat. Maxine reached for her hand and gripped it tightly.

"We'll stay at a hotel tonight," Maxine said. "Let's go in and pack some clothes for work tomorrow."

Maxine opened the car door and got out, but Betina didn't budge. Maxine opened the passenger's door again and told her to turn off the car. "Come inside, baby," she said. "We'll get this fixed."

They walked up to the porch holding hands as Maxine's brain attempted to process what exactly had happened. If this discontinuation of service thing was a mistake, she'd kick up a stink like the City Public Service agency had never seen before!

She took Betina's keys and went to unlock the front door, but it was open already.

"You didn't lock the door when you left?" Maxine asked her.

Betina began to cry again.

The house was eerily quiet and hot from having the air conditioner off all day. It was still light enough inside to see, but that wouldn't last much longer. Maxine got one of the pre-packed gym bags she had fixed earlier in the week and tossed in a brush, hair dryer and a few toiletries for good measure. Packed and ready to go, Maxine went looking for Betina, only to find her standing by the sofa with a handful of envelopes.

"Go throw a few things together," Maxine said.

Betina handed her the pile of envelopes and then went into the bedroom. Maxine set her gym bag near the front door and looked at the mail Betina had given her. There were statements and bills with postmarks that were two months old already. She opened the front door wider in order to let in what little daylight remained. As Maxine began to open the envelopes, she could see where the water bill, electric bill, Visa, MasterCard, Discover, Diners Club, cable bill, car payments, insurance premiums, magazine subscriptions, and even a renewal notice for Maxine's medical license were all in need of immediate attention. There were overdue notices, cancellation notices and discontinuation of services acknowledgments. The more envelopes she opened, the more shocked and angry she became.

Maxine went over to the sofa to sit down and compose herself. Her eyes zoomed in and settled on the pile of circulars and junk mail that was on the coffee table. She went through each piece of mail and found a bill for the newspaper and one for the quarterly pest control service they used. The rest of the mail was unimportant. She glanced at her watch and realized Betina had been in the other room a long time. Maxine was still stunned and trying to come to terms with her confusion and anger over this. How could Betina have let such a thing happen? *My medical license!* Maxine thought. Without physically seeing or receiving a notice from the state, Maxine wouldn't have remembered on her own when exactly her license came up for renewal. She still had ten days to get it renewed, but just the thought of not having it taken care of in a timely manner was unthinkable. That was the one piece of correspondence that had upset her the most, even as she sat in a hot, dark house, contemplating the predicament they were now in. *I might have to drive to Austin tomorrow and deliver cash in person to get it renewed!* she thought.

"Are you packed yet?" Maxine called. She made an effort to keep her voice neutral even though she was fuming inside. When Betina didn't answer, Maxine went looking for her.

She stopped in the doorway of their bedroom and saw Betina curled up on the bed in a fetal position. Her shoulders moved as if she were crying again, but Maxine couldn't hear any sounds coming from her. She crawled on the bed and snuggled up behind her. Betina's sobs turned more vocal at Maxine's initial touch. Seeing Betina this way made Maxine's heart swell. She tried to swallow the huge lump in her throat as she tugged on Betina's arm and made her turn over so she could hold her.

"Please, don't do this, baby," Maxine whispered.

Betina put her hands tightly over her face again as her body continued to be consumed by sobs.

"Please, baby," Maxine whispered through her own tears. "Don't. It'll be okay. I promise." She pulled Betina closer and rubbed her cheek against her hair. They were both warm and beginning to sweat now.

Maxine no longer cared about the power being off or her medical license on the verge of expiring. All she wanted to do right then was help Betina get past this bout of hysteria they were both trapped in at the moment. She started with a string of light kisses on the top of Betina's head and then down along her temple. She eventually managed to pry Betina's hands away from her tearstained face and kissed her nose and the side of her mouth.

"Please don't cry like this, baby," Maxine whispered in an emotionally fragile voice.

Holy moly it's hot in here, she thought as she held Betina close. Eventually the sobbing stopped and became a series of sniffs and hiccups. Between trying to catch her breath and dabbing her runny nose on her blouse, Betina tried to get control of herself.

"I . . ." she started. "I . . . don't . . ."

"Shhh," Maxine whispered. "It's okay."

"How . . . can . . . you . . . say that?" Betina asked as she closed her eyes and took another series of raggedy breaths. "We're . . . sweating . . . in the . . . dark . . . because of . . . me."

Maxine kissed the top of her damp head again. "We're staying at a hotel tonight as soon as we get an overnight bag packed up for you."

"Then let's do it," Betina said. She sat up and brushed tears away with the back of her hand. Once she was standing up and appeared to be gathering clothes to put in a suitcase, Maxine returned to the living room to find all the unpaid bills.

Just as an afterthought, Maxine walked down to the mailbox near the street. She felt a sense of dread when she opened it up and saw how full it was. Maxine took out an armload of circulars, magazines, and a pile of envelopes before closing the lid. She sorted through as much as she could by the last light of day on her way back to the house. She added the new junk mail to the other stack on the coffee table and asked herself again how this could have happened.

During the five years they had been together, Betina had always tended to their household bills. They had a joint checking account where they both deposited a certain amount of money each month. *If she hasn't paid the car payments, then the house payment probably hasn't been made in weeks either,* Maxine realized.

She went out to her car to get a flashlight and returned to the house to locate the coupon payment books for both cars and the house. She found them all in the desk drawer by the stereo. Maxine bundled everything together and stuck it all in her gym bag.

Several minutes later Betina came out of the bedroom with a suitcase in each hand and a giant wad of tissues stuck in her bra. She set her bags down by the front door and plucked out a tissue to blow her nose on.

"I'm ready," she announced.

Maxine offered a tired smile as she picked up her keys. Not wanting to make a bad situation any worse, she attempted to lighten things up a bit. Betina wasn't crying now and Maxine hoped to keep it that way.

"Let me guess," Maxine said. "One suitcase has shoes and the other has your makeup."

"I'll have you know," Betina said with a stuffy nose, "one bag has makeup *and* shoes."

"I see."

"I'll need choices when I decide what I'm going to wear tomorrow."

"I know."

Maxine picked up her gym bag and one of Betina's suitcases. Stooping over as if having trouble carrying it, she said, "Yikes. This one must have the shoes and makeup in it."

Chapter Eleven

Maxine sat at the desk in their room at the Holiday Inn and glanced toward the bed where Betina was asleep. She ran her fingers through the front of her hair and couldn't believe how long this day had been. A tinge of anxiety kept Maxine on edge. As she wrote out checks for bill after bill and licked the flap on over fifteen envelopes, she was finally able to come to terms with what made Betina completely disregard this particular responsibility. Maxine had an idea why everything had suddenly changed, but she wasn't eager to admit what her skills and instincts as a physician were telling her.

As she stared down at the checkbook, there were other fleeting thoughts that crossed her mind. Was there even any money left in their joint account? Could Betina have failed to pay the bills because all the money was gone—perhaps used for some sinister reason? Maxine had a monthly direct deposit of four thousand dollars going into their joint account for whatever bills needed to be paid or for any miscellaneous household expenses or emergencies. Betina contributed a thousand dollars a month to the same account. They both had their own personal checking accounts as well as other financial resources, including mutual funds, stocks, and bonds. Twice a year they used whatever was left over in the joint account to go on a nice vacation, so it was more or less used as a "slush fund." Maxine made a lot more money than Betina did, but they both contributed a percentage of their annual earnings in order to support the lifestyle they had chosen.

Maxine found the phone number for the bank on the front of a check. She called the number to get a balance for that particular checking account. They used the same PIN number for everything, so Maxine was able to get the information easily. She breathed a sigh of relief after hearing the balance.

"Sixteen thousand, eight hundred thirty-five dollars and fifty-two cents," the automated voice reported.

Maxine wrote down the amount and was ashamed at how relieved she felt at hearing there was still a nice balance in there. *So what were you thinking?* she wondered. *That your lover had squandered the household kitty? On what? Shoes and makeup? Lotto tickets? The ponies? Booze? Other women? Just what the hell were you thinking?*

She glanced over at the bed again and felt a twinge in her heart at the sight of Betina sleeping so peacefully. Even though Betina's eyes were puffy from crying, she was still a beautiful woman. *So why didn't she pay the bills?* Maxine wondered. *It's a busy time of year for her at work with proms coming up and spring weddings. But she's always been busy and she's always taken the time to keep our monthly expenses and needs in order. So what's different now? What's happened to change that?*

"Forget it," she mumbled to herself. "You already know why."

Maxine took out her cell phone and her address book to look up Joey's number. As Betina's twin brother and business partner, Joey Abbott should have firsthand insight into any weird behavior Betina had been displaying. She found Joey's number and went to the bathroom and closed the door. Since her cell phone and pager were paid

84

for from the office budget in her medical practice, at least she didn't have to worry about being available for her patients. She dialed Joey's number and could hear deep, male laughter in the background when he answered the phone.

"Joey, it's Maxine. I'm sorry to call so late." She looked at her watch and saw that it was nine-thirty already. To her it was late.

"Maxie! It's good to hear from you! What's the occasion?"

It sounded like he was having a party. The usual thumping bass that accompanied "gay-boy" music was loud and she could hear several men talking in the background.

"If this is a bad time—"

"No. Of course not," he said. "What's up? You never call just to say hi. Is everything okay?"

She heard him close a door and it instantly became quieter on the other end of the phone.

"It should be by tomorrow," she said, thinking about having to jump through a few hoops the next day in order to get the power restored at home. Maxine suddenly realized how tired she felt. Emotional upheavals were just so exhausting.

"Is Betina okay?" Joey asked. "You're sounding weird. What's the matter?"

Maxine took a deep breath. "I was wondering if you've noticed any changes in your sister lately. You spend more awake time with her than I do."

Joey's voice took on a more serious tone. "I've actually been meaning to call you about that. I've been putting it off for some reason, though."

That same icy fear that Maxine had experienced earlier in the evening was back again. "Tell me about it," she said. "What have you noticed?"

"Well, for one thing, she can't get to work on time anymore. For a while there she was missing appointments and having to reschedule clients. It was terrible. Now I call her every morning when I get up just so I know she's awake. Sometimes I have to call her three or four times before she finally gets up, though. And you know that's not like her."

Maxine listened to him and couldn't believe he was describing the person she knew. Betina was never one to lounge around in bed. She was a morning person and usually got up early even if she didn't have to work. Betina also enjoyed her profession and the relationships she had with her clients. Maxine didn't like what she was hearing, but this new information only served to reinforce her suspicions about what was going on.

"I finally stopped nagging her about getting up each morning," Joey continued. "Now I make her take the phone to the bathroom and turn on the shower so I can hear it running. I know that once I get her out of bed and walking around a little, she'll more than likely stay up and get ready for work."

When Maxine left for the office each morning, she assumed Betina was getting on with her day like she always had. Maxine felt ashamed for not knowing any of this about her lover and wondered how long Joey would have waited before saying something to her. *If this fiasco with the power company hadn't happened,* she thought, *when would I have found out about this on my own?*

"How long has this been going on?" she asked quietly.

"It's gotten really bad over the last month or so."

A month, Maxine thought. *Where the hell have you been during that month, Dr. Weston?*

"How is she when she gets to work?" Maxine asked.

"She's tired all the time," Joey said. "She even naps in between appointments."

"Naps in between appointments," Maxine repeated. "You're not kidding, are you?"

"I thought you two were just having too much wild sex and it was wearing her out."

Sex, Maxine thought. *When was the last time we made love?* Maxine couldn't even remember.

"But now you're making me think that wild sex isn't the problem."

"No," Maxine admitted, then suddenly something else came to her. "Who pays the bills at the shop? You or Betina?"

"She does. I do the ordering of supplies and equipment. We take care of the salon's expenses before drawing a salary each month."

Maxine decided not to clue him in on the possibility that the power to the Hair Today Salon could be turned off any day now if Betina was the one responsible for paying the bills there. She would ask Betina about it in the morning. If the salon's finances with bill collectors were in the same situation that hers and Betina's were in, then Maxine would help her take care of it before Joey found out anything. It was very possible that there were a pile of bills at the salon that had been grossly neglected for a while now, too.

"Okay," Maxine said. "You've been helpful. I'll try and make sure she gets more rest."

"Thanks. Her clients and I would appreciate it."

After putting in a request for a wake-up call with the front desk, Maxine took a quick shower and crawled into bed. She snuggled against Betina and kissed her bare back before slipping her arm around her waist spoon-fashion. Betina slowly turned over and kissed Maxine's cheek and shoulder.

"You still love me?" Betina whispered in a small, sleepy voice.

"Of course I still love you. Come here. Let me hold you."

"Even though I'm an idiot?"

Maxine smiled. "You're not an idiot."

"I feel like one."

Maxine had left the bathroom light on and the door cracked a little. She brushed Betina's hair away from her forehead and kissed her.

"I'm going to make an appointment for you tomorrow," Maxine said.

"What kind of appointment?"

"You're showing signs of depression, baby." Saying it out loud made Maxine's eyes fill with tears. It was out in the open now. There was no one to blame and no way to "fix things" on their own. Depression was serious and something that a professional could treat and help with.

"Depression?" Betina repeated. "Where did that come from?"

"It's possible I'm wrong," Maxine said, "but I don't think so. That's why I want you to get a complete physical tomorrow and then a psychological evaluation when—"

"So you think I'm crazy?"

Maxine hugged her. "Did you hear me utter that word? Nooo. I see women all day long who are pregnant and would rather not be, or who experience signs of depression after their babies are born. It's nothing to be ashamed of and it's much more common than people think."

"Well, I'm not pregnant and there won't be any babies," Betina said as she pulled away from her. "Spit don't make babies, as they say. Jeez. I forget to tend to the mail and you're sending me off to a shrink!"

Maxine hugged her again. "It's not just the mail. What about all the sleeping you've been doing? I've even noticed you leaving the house without putting on makeup."

"What? When have I ever forgotten to look my best?"

"You look great no matter what you do."

"Answer my question."

Maxine didn't say anything. She didn't like where this was going.

"Thought so," Betina said. "Can't think of anything, can you?"

Maxine took a slow, deep breath. She didn't want to get into this now. They both needed to be up early and it had already been an evening overwrought with emotion.

"I'm not crazy," Betina said.

"Depression has nothing to do with being crazy."

"But seeing a shrink does."

"What? Why are you—"

"How many normal people go to a shrink?"

Maxine had not expected this type of outburst. Betina was a reasonable, intelligent woman.

"I can't believe you're—"

"Shut up and hold me," Betina said in a small voice.

Maxine pulled her closer and felt a cool teardrop hit her shoulder. They were quiet for a moment. Maxine held her and tried to regroup and think about her next attempt at convincing Betina to at least give seeking professional help a try.

"It'll be okay, baby," Maxine whispered.

"I don't wanna be depressed."

"I know." She kissed the side of Betina's head. "They've got some good drugs out there now that'll make you feel better."

"There's a drug for everything, I suppose."

"Depression is serious. If it goes untreated, it only gets worse. If it's undertreated, then it'll likely return. So you'll go to the appointment if I make it?"

"If I see a shrink, I don't want it to be someone you know."

"I don't understand what you mean by that," Maxine said. "Any physician you see wouldn't share confidential information with me or anyone else."

"I don't like shrinks."

"That's fine. You don't have to like them. You can even pick a psychiatrist or psychologist on your own. I don't care who you see. But depression is a serious thing, babe. It's affecting how you function in your everyday life. I want you to see someone immediately and get evaluated."

"Don't use that tone with me," Betina said with a sniff.

Maxine smiled and finally felt as though she had made some progress with her. She gave Betina a tender kiss on the lips and reassured her once again that everything would be fine.

They fell asleep holding each other.

Chapter Twelve

Maxine woke up to the phone ringing on the nightstand. It was early and she needed to be in surgery that morning, but she and Betina had a lot to take care of before their day was to begin.

"I'll take a shower first," Maxine said after giving Betina a kiss on her shoulder. Rolling out of bed, she found her gym bag and noticed that Betina still wasn't awake yet. Standing at the side of the bed, Maxine leaned over and kissed her on the cheek. "Come on, baby. Take a shower with me."

"No, you go first," Betina mumbled with her eyes still closed.

Maxine tossed the covers off and gave Betina's thigh a hearty shake. "Get up. We're taking a shower."

She couldn't stop thinking about the things Joey had said about Betina's new morning routine. *We've got too much to do today*, Maxine thought. *We both need to get going.*

Betina got out of bed and stormed to the bathroom, slamming

the door. Maxine gathered up soap and shampoo and followed her in as soon as she heard a flush and then the shower running. Maxine got into the shower with her and started washing Betina's back. To her surprise, Betina began to cry again.

Maxine turned her around and gave her a hug as the shower sprayed down on them. *This isn't the Betina I know*, she thought. *I need to get her an appointment with someone today. This can't wait.*

"It'll be okay, baby," Maxine said, her voice low and hollow as it echoed off the shower walls. "Let's get finished in here and talk about what we need to do today."

They soaped each other up and changing positions in the small shower. Maxine closed her eyes and let the spray hit her face and hair as it washed off the soap and shampoo.

"Mmm," she said. Betina's tongue circled one of her nipples before taking it into her mouth. Maxine felt an immediate rush of warmth spread through her body. Betina stood up and kissed her deeply as the water continued to pelt them. She moved her hand down to Maxine's stomach and caressed her before slipping two fingers inside. The kiss deepened and Betina sucked Maxine's tongue into her mouth.

Maxine's hands automatically went to Betina's breasts where she rubbed her nipples with her thumbs. Betina was persistent and encouraged Maxine to open her legs. She kissed her again and used her tongue in a suggestive in-and-out dance that made Maxine's knees weak. When Betina parted her with long, talented fingers, Maxine felt a pulsating mixture of heat and pleasure. Every fiber of her being was centered on Betina's touch and her exquisite ability to make Maxine forget anything and everything at that moment. Maxine moved against her and deepened the kiss, searching for and capturing Betina's tongue as it helped tease her to orgasm.

Maxine threw her head back and let the shower spray strip the remnants of soap and shampoo from her body, where eventually all that remained was the warm glow of passion.

⋘⋙

Maxine sat on the edge of the bed to put her socks on. Having skipped dinner the night before, she was hungry and knew she'd have to get something to eat before going to the hospital. She had a hysterectomy scheduled at eight and a cesarean afterward. There would be no time to catch a meal until after those two surgeries were completed.

She watched Betina piddle around the room in her black lace bra and panties. Maxine wasn't sure how to bring up the unpleasantness that awaited them, but they were working against the clock already.

"Come here and sit beside me for a minute," Maxine said. She patted the bed and took a deep breath. "Two things," she said. "Someone needs to take care of getting the electricity turned back on today."

Betina hung her head and nodded.

"I'm in surgery this morning and—"

"I'll take care of it," Betina said with a sniff. "It's my screw-up."

"What's your appointment schedule look like today?"

"It's full. I'll just reschedule those I can."

Maxine now had doubts about Betina's judgment when it came to work issues and her commitment to her clients. Most of them scheduled appointments with her weeks in advance. Maxine found it hard to focus on what she now knew about her lover, especially since there were so many things that were normal about what Betina did and the things she said. The unusual behavior was sporadic and she seemed to be able to function quite well when prodded.

"So you'll take care of getting the power turned back on today?" Maxine asked.

"Yes."

"Okay. Then I have one more thing to ask." Maxine finished putting on her sneakers before continuing. "It's my understanding that you're the one who pays the bills at the shop. Is that true?"

Betina let out a little gasp and then jumped up off the bed. She went to the closet where all her clothes were hanging and whipped through the four outfits on the hangers, inspecting each one carefully.

"Betina," Maxine said.

The clunking sound of wooden hangers smacking against each other over and over again as Betina gave each outfit another thorough inspection was almost as annoying for Maxine as her not answering.

"Betina," Maxine said again a bit louder.

"I can't decide what to wear today."

Maxine could hear the tears in her voice. She got up from the bed and went to her, taking Betina in her arms. She held her for a long time while they cried together there in front of the open closet.

A while later, Maxine whispered, "Wear the turquoise dress and the white sandals. That's my favorite. You look great in that outfit."

Betina sniffed. "I was thinking something a bit slinkier. Might get the power turned on faster."

"More like the power *man* turned on faster," Maxine said with a smile. She gave Betina's butt a nice pat. "Get dressed, baby. We need to check out and get going."

Maxine was ready and had her clothes from the day before stuffed inside her gym bag. She sat on the side of the rumpled bed and watched Betina finish dressing.

"This is what we'll do, babe," Maxine said. "I'll go with you to the shop this morning and we'll collect all the mail and all the bills. I'll help you pay them tonight and we'll make whatever arrangements need to be made to keep Joey in the dark about this."

"Pun intended?" Betina asked with a sniff.

Maxine smiled and felt a familiar tugging in her heart. *God, I love this woman*, she thought.

❧

93

Maxine parked beside Betina's car in the Hair Today parking lot. The sun was just beginning to come up, but Maxine had about forty-five minutes before she needed to be at the hospital to see her first patient. She followed Betina inside and helped her turn on the lights.

"Where do you usually put the mail?" Maxine asked. Remembering how full their own mailbox had been, Maxine went back outside and emptied the shop's mailbox as well. She carried in a pile of envelopes and catalogs, sorting through them slowly so as not to miss anything. A few minutes later Betina came out of the back room with a stack of catalogs, circulars and envelopes of all sizes that was almost too high for her to carry on her own. Maxine tried to hide her shock by staying busy going through her half of the stack a piece at a time. When she was finally finished, she held out her hand for the envelopes Betina had found. Maxine then quickly sorted through the stack of catalogs, flyers, and circulars that Betina had already gone through and was satisfied they had extracted all the bills.

"I'll keep these," Maxine said as she combined both piles of envelopes. "We'll take care of them when I get home tonight."

"I can do it today," Betina said in a small, teary voice.

Maxine kissed her tenderly on the lips. "We'll do it together this evening when I get home from work." She pointed to the other mail sitting on the counter. "Why don't you go through the rest of this and then make a list of clients you need to reschedule today? Give them a call at a decent hour."

Betina nodded. The tears in her eyes and the lost, bewildered expression on her beautiful face made Maxine want to do everything possible to make things better for her again.

Maxine was back in her office by noon and had a waiting room full of patients when she arrived.

"I just took these within the last three minutes," Mona said as she handed her four messages.

"And a good afternoon to you, too, Mona," Maxine said on her way to her office.

"Oh. Sorry. Yeah. Good afternoon, Dr. Weston."

She handed Mona the stack of envelopes and a crisp twenty-dollar bill. "These need stamps and have to go out today, please. Oh, and I need for you to call the Texas State Board of Medical Examiners and see what I have to do to get my license renewed—today."

"Wow," Mona said. "Nothing like waiting until the last minute."

"It only *takes* a minute if you wait until the last minute," Maxine said. She shuffled through the messages and stopped at the one from Betina. In Mona's slanted, loopy script were the words "Mission accomplished. All systems go." She called Betina's cell phone and could tell she was in the car when she answered.

"So we have power at home now?" Maxine asked.

"Yes. I'm on my way back to work. I'll need to stay late this evening. Some of my appointments couldn't be switched to another day."

"Call me back when you get to work," Maxine said. "I need to know your schedule for tomorrow so I can get an appointment for your physical."

There was silence on the other end of the phone.

"Betina?"

"Yeah, yeah. I'll call you later with that info."

"Don't blow me off. I'm serious about this."

"I know. I've gotta go. I'll see you tonight."

Maxine returned the other three phone calls and then was ready to see some patients. She decided she could use an ordinary day at the office.

Maxine didn't get home until after six. She saw a small pickup in the driveway and had no idea who it could be until Ann Kingston introduced herself.

"I'm sorry I'm late," Maxine said. "I guess Betina isn't here yet either. How long have you been waiting?"

"Just a few minutes," Ann said. She was tall and thin, with wild, frizzy brown hair sprinkled with gray. She reminded Maxine of a fifty-year-old hippie with her worn, faded jeans and yellow pocket T-shirt.

"I think I've seen you around," Maxine said, "but we've never met." She led the way up the sidewalk and unlocked the front door. A horrendous stench hit them the moment the door was opened. "Whoa!" Maxine said. "What in the world is that *smell?*"

Her anger returned as she trudged through the living room and dining room. When Maxine got to the kitchen door, she found the two garbage bags that had been sitting there for several days already and four new ones with everything that had spoiled in the refrigerator after the power had been turned off.

With her hands on her hips, Maxine said, "Well, isn't *this* embarrassing!"

The new full trash bags weren't closed up, but had been placed alongside the other two older and riper ones.

"We've had a recent problem with the power company," Maxine explained.

"Let's get these outside," Ann said. She found the ties for the trash bags on the kitchen counter and began closing up the opened bags. She picked up one in each hand and carried them out of the kitchen.

Maxine followed Ann's lead and tied off the other opened trash bags and carried them outside. She saw Ann toss her two bags in the back of her truck.

"We'll just set 'em in there," Ann said. "I'll get rid of them for you."

By the time Maxine got back in the house again, Ann was on her way out with the last of the trash.

Maxine didn't let her embarrassment interfere with getting Ann Kingston lined up as their housekeeper. She liked the way Ann just pitched in to help. She even found an air freshener in her box of cleaning supplies in her truck and set it on the kitchen counter. Maxine got them both something to drink—sodas, wine, and bottled water being the only things left in the fridge.

Maxine gave her a tour of the house and got some feedback on what Ann did for her other customers. Thirty minutes later, Maxine gave her a key to the house and agreed to leave a check on the dining table two Thursdays a month.

"I usually call the day before as a reminder," Ann said. "So if you have anything in particular you want done, just let me know then or leave a note."

"Thanks," Maxine said. "You've been a big help already. Things aren't usually this bad here. Really." *Holy moly, how embarrassing!*

After Ann left, Maxine went to the mailbox to get the day's mail. She glanced at her watch and wondered what time Betina would be home.

Chapter Thirteen

Maxine ordered a pizza and worked on the other article while she waited for Betina. The pizza and Betina arrived within moments of each other.

"See?" Betina said to Maxine after she paid the pizza guy. "I knew you could order one all by your little self."

Maxine laughed and was glad to see Betina in a good mood. "So how was your day? How were things with the power man?"

"I had to go downtown and pay cash first," Betina said, "so that was a major inconvenience. Parking downtown is next to impossible anyway. Then I had to stand in a special line with the other delinquent customers, so that was a bit degrading. While I was there I took care of the bill for the shop, too." She got them something to drink and then slid pizza slices onto their plates. "You talked to Joey yesterday," Betina said. "Why didn't you tell me?"

"I was worried about you, and so is your brother."

"How much did you tell him?"

"I didn't tell him anything. I did all the asking. Why?"

Betina shrugged. "He was pissy about me having to reschedule my clients today."

"I thought Joey was always pissy."

Betina smiled. "Well . . . yeah. He is. So I guess I meant to say *extra* pissy."

Maxine looked at her over the open pizza box. "Think about it this way. The fewer clients you have, the less money the salon brings in. Joey's worried about his wallet, too."

Betina nodded and looked down at her plate. "So I've been letting everyone down. Not just you."

"You haven't let me down. We'll get past this, baby. Now what's your schedule like tomorrow? I want you to get a physical as soon as possible."

"Full. And the day after, too."

Maxine took a deep breath. "I can get an appointment for you after hours. How late are you working tomorrow?"

"I told you once already that I don't want to see someone you know."

Maxine didn't want to argue. "I don't care who you go to for the physical, just make sure you do it soon. Like this week. *Soon.*"

"Yeah, yeah, yeah."

Maxine shook her head. "Don't yeah, yeah, yeah me. I'm serious and *this* is serious."

"Okay, okay. I have a doctor in mind already."

"Who is it?"

"I thought you said you didn't care who I went to?"

"You're right. I'm sorry."

"Anyway, I was thinking about giving Dr. Abernathy a call."

Maxine nearly choked on her pizza. "Your old pediatrician?"

Betina threw her head back and laughed.

"He's retired!"

"He was my doctor for a very long time."

"You're a little old for a pediatrician, don't you think?"

"I trust him," Betina said. "And he won't tell you a thing."

"He's retired," Maxine said again. "He can't see patients now."

Betina smiled and winked at her. "I'm just messing with you, darlin'. I promise to make an appointment with someone this week, okay?"

They finished paying the bills for the Hair Today Salon at the dining room table after dinner. Betina insisted on writing them all out, but seemed to like having Maxine there beside her asking questions and being attentive. Maxine had never taken an interest in the "behind the scenes" details about how Betina and Joey's business was handled. There was obviously much more to it than cutting hair and paying a few bills.

"Who keeps the books?" Maxine asked.

"I used to, but now we have an accountant called the Tax Princess. I keep all our paperwork in a big box and turn it over to him every February. Some of the stuff has to be done quarterly."

Maxine glanced at a statement for hair products and supplies and said, "You could sure save a lot of money by paying these bills sooner."

Betina cut her eyes over at her. "You sound like Joey."

"Well, look at this," Maxine said. She pointed to a figure on the statement. "If you pay it when the bill comes in—"

"I know what the bill says."

Maxine nodded slowly and set the piece of paper back down on the stack. "Is there anything I can do to help?"

"Be supportive and not criticize?" Betina suggested.

Maxine smiled. "I can do that." She leaned back in her chair and then had another idea. "Are you finished eating?"

"Yes."

"Then watch this," Maxine said. She closed the pizza box that still contained four slices. "This is me putting leftover pizza away."

She picked up the box and took it to the kitchen. Since the refrigerator was empty because of the power outage the day before, the box fit easily on the bare shelf. Maxine returned to the dining room and draped her arms around Betina's neck.

Betina turned her head to kiss her and whispered, "Who said you couldn't be trained?"

They changed the linen on the bed and took a quick shower together. Maxine felt a sense of relief at Betina's playfulness as the evening began to wind down. She spoke at length to each of Maxine's breasts while lathering them with soap and seemed more like her old self than Maxine remembered her being over the last few weeks.

"Clean sheets," Betina said while slipping into bed naked. "These four-hundred-thread-count sheets make me think I'm floating on a cloud."

Maxine got into bed and also liked the "right out of the dryer" smell and feel of fresh sheets against her skin.

"Put some lotion on me, baby," Betina said.

"That vanilla pudding stuff from Victoria's Secret?"

Maxine sat up and opened the jar Betina gave her. She pulled the covers away from Betina's body and smiled at the way she brought her legs up to be pampered. Maxine enjoyed rubbing the lotion on her lover almost as much as Betina liked the stimulation and attention. Touching those smooth, soft legs gave her a sudden thrill. She rubbed the scented lotion on the inside of Betina's calf and leaned close enough so her left nipple grazed the side of her knee.

"You have no idea how much I like this," Betina said. Arching her back and gripping the sides of her pillow, she made the most delightful noise in the back of her throat.

"You'd be wrong there," Maxine said. She gently scooped more of the lotion on her fingers and applied it to the inside of Betina's right thigh. Betina opened her legs so Maxine could have better access.

"Do I need a trim?"

Maxine glanced down at the pale tuft of pubic hair and ran the tip of her finger over it. "Looks fine to me."

"Okay then. More lotion. You're not finished."

Maxine dipped her fingers into the jar again and began rubbing them on Betina's other thigh, slowly moving her way up. The longer she touched her soft warm skin, the more aroused Maxine became. After several moments of working the lotion in, she moved her hand down and began to rub along the top of Betina's foot, then slowly up her leg and over the knee in a sensuous caress. She kissed the side of Betina's mid thigh and released a deep sigh when Betina touched Maxine's breast.

As if they were reading each other's thoughts, Betina slid her feet down and opened her legs more while Maxine continued to kiss her thigh and run her hand up the inside of her leg. Betina's hand went from Maxine's breast to her hair, eventually urging her head closer. Maxine moved between Betina's legs and settled in comfortably. She opened Betina up with her fingers and then lightly teased her with her tongue. Wet, warm, and smelling of blueberry soap and Dream Angel lotion, Maxine sucked Betina's clitoris into her mouth just long enough to get her attention. She flicked her tongue around it and was surprised at how big it got so quickly.

"Guess what?" Maxine whispered before taking the pea-sized clit into her mouth again.

"Is she out?" Betina asked excitedly. "Is she?!"

"Yes," Maxine said.

The more she teased her, the larger it began to swell.

"Oh, baby," Betina said as she began moving her hips. She gripped Maxine's hair and was ready to come. "Your Betina will have a *gooood* time tonight." She wrapped her legs around Maxine and began to grind against her. "How big is she? How big . . ."

Maxine sucked on her clitoris again and the bucking and groaning began almost immediately. By the time Betina had wrung the last ounce of pleasure from the encounter, Maxine had also come once just from listening to her.

"Oh, baby . . . come here," Betina said weakly. She tugged on Maxine's ear with the last of her strength.

Maxine used the sheet to wipe her mouth off and then rose up on her arms. She let one of her hard nipples graze Betina's throbbing clit, causing both of them to gasp from the pleasant sensation.

"Oh, baby. Do that again," Betina said breathlessly. "Please . . ."

Maxine had been thinking the same thing. She took her time rubbing her breast into Betina's wet, throbbing center.

"That feels *sooo* good," Betina said. "Can you feel how big she is?"

It still amazed Maxine how Betina could become so obsessed with the size of her clitoris at any given time. Raising herself up with her arms again, Maxine repositioned herself on top of her.

"Ohhh . . . this feels incredible, too," Betina said. She put her arms around Maxine's back and kissed her with such passion that their bodies began a new writhing dance. Betina wrapped her legs around Maxine's and latched on for another thrilling ride. They were both truly exhausted by the time they came together a few minutes later.

"That was nice, baby," Betina whispered sleepily. Nestled in Maxine's arms, she barely had enough energy to kiss her shoulder.

"Something in that lotion makes you wild," Maxine said.

"Part of Victoria's secret maybe."

Maxine was too tired to comment, but did manage a small hug.

"I felt fine today," Betina said. "No naps and I took care of the mail here and at the shop."

"That's good," Maxine mumbled. She was drifting off to sleep and could feel her arms relaxing.

"I think that little bout of depression might be over."

"You . . . promised to see . . . a doctor . . . this . . ."

The next thing Maxine knew, it was morning already and the alarm clock went off.

Chapter Fourteen

Maxine hadn't been at the restaurant very long when Elaine arrived. They placed their breakfast orders and tended to their coffees.

"You can sure tell it's tourist season," Elaine said. "Traffic was awful this morning. Lots of license plates from Mexico. They're probably up for the Easter holiday."

"You don't need an excuse for being late, Dr. Marcaluso," Maxine said with a smile. "Besides, are tourists even awake at this hour?"

"Oh, by the way, my mom told me you and I are both scheduled to be at the clinic next week. That should be fun."

"Make sure she lines up a drug rep that believes in feeding us well," Maxine said. "None of those cheap bean and cheese tacos again. Hmm. I'm wondering if IHOP has takeout for breakfast."

"She knows how to keep us happy. I'm sure that's covered already."

"We make it sound like we're only there for the free food," Maxine noted.

Elaine shrugged. "I like spending time with my mother in a professional setting, but free food certainly cheers me up while I'm there."

Out of habit, Maxine checked her pager and cell phone to make sure they were both on and working. "Maybe she should get your sister-the-lawyer to offer some *pro bono* legal advice and just make those free clinic days a nice family affair."

"Oh, puhleeze. My sister-the-lawyer doesn't do anything for free."

Maxine stirred her coffee to cool it down faster. "I was wondering about your referral list for psychiatrists."

"What about it?"

"Could you have someone in your office fax it over to me today?"

Elaine pulled out a small tablet with a pen attached to it. "I can't remember anything if I don't write it down these days."

"How many names are on the referral list?" Maxine asked.

"I have about five I use. Depends on what type of insurance the patient has. Most of my referrals are adolescents. Some psychiatrists work better with depressed teenagers than others, though. Acne sure takes its toll on a kid's self-esteem, but we've gotten some excellent results. Why? Are you unhappy with the ones you've been using?"

"No. It's just good to see what's out there."

"Did something happen with one of your referrals?"

"No! I'm just curious about who you're using these days."

Maxine had hopes of hooking Betina up with a psychiatrist that none of their friends knew, so having Elaine's list would be helpful. If Betina was worried about seeing a psychiatrist, Maxine wanted to do whatever she could to make things easier for her.

"You two still on for a Spurs game next week?"

"Uh," Maxine said. "Maybe you should write one of those notes for me or I'll never remember to ask. I'll get back with you tomorrow."

⌇⌇⌇

After work, Maxine arrived home in time to help Betina bring in the groceries.

"I had to buy a lot of extra stuff since the power outage spoiled most of the things in the fridge," Betina said as she took two bags in each hand from the trunk of the car. "Mustard, mayo, steak sauce. It made me feel poor each time I opened that danged refrigerator."

Maxine got the last four bags out and closed the trunk. "Did you see a doctor today?"

Betina gave her a curious look. "I worked today."

"Then did you at least call someone for an appointment?"

Betina stepped up the pace and reached the front door first. She didn't bother holding the door open for Maxine and let it slam shut just before Maxine got to the porch.

Okay, Maxine thought. *I see where this is going. Now I'll have to be "the bitch" again in order to get things back on track.*

When she entered the kitchen she found Betina kneeling in front of the refrigerator putting items away. Maxine handed perishables to her from the bags she had carried in, but there wasn't any other interaction between them until all the groceries were put away.

Finally, Maxine said, "So you didn't call and make an appointment like I asked you to."

"Why are you doing this?" Betina asked. She was crying again.

"I'm doing this because I love you and I'm worried about you."

"Maybe you should mind your own business."

Maxine glanced down at her to see if she was serious before saying, "Your health *is* my business, so don't even go there."

"Can't you see that I'm better? I'm checking the mail, I'm doing the shopping, I'm getting ready to put some laundry on, I'm—"

"This isn't about a daily routine, Betina. It's not about laundry and mail. It's about fatigue, stress, anger—"

"I'm doing *better*!" she yelled.

The outburst seemed to shock them both into an uncomfortable silence.

"Sure you are," Maxine said dryly, then turned and went to her study to work on her paper.

Having incorporated her new notes and research into the article, Maxine was beginning to feel good about how it was shaping up. She took a lot of pride in her scholarly activities and hoped the new manuscript on hormone replacement therapy would soon find a home in a peer review publication. She printed out the latest draft and decided she was too tired to go over it again. Her eyes would be fresher in the morning.

There was a light knock on her door. Betina came in holding a piece of paper.

"Do you know a Dr. Fredrick Miller?" she asked.

"Yes," Maxine said. "He's a fine internist. Did his residency at—"

"Okay," Betina said, cutting her off. She glanced down at the paper again. "How about a Dr. Yolanda Ramirez?"

Maxine thought for a moment, but couldn't recall the name. "No, I've never heard of her."

"Okay. Good. I'll make an appointment with her tomorrow. You happy now?"

Maxine offered a tired smile. "You can sure be a little shit sometimes. Anyone ever tell you that?"

"Not in so many words. You didn't have any dinner tonight. There's cold pizza in the fridge if you're hungry. I'm going to bed."

Maxine didn't say anything. She watched Betina stand there with fresh tears in her eyes. As they looked at each other, she felt that familiar tugging in her heart.

"Why can't you see that I'm doing better?" Betina whispered.

Maxine felt tears of her own on the way. "Why can't you see that you're not? This isn't about picking up the dry cleaning and checking the mail, baby. There's a lot more than that going on."

"Oh, hell," Betina said, and began to cry harder. "I forgot to pick up the dry cleaning today!"

Maxine got up from her desk and took Betina in her arms.

"I made a list and everything."

Maxine wasn't sure what to do anymore. She didn't want to alienate her by continuing to harp on the "go to the doctor" thing, but she needed to make Betina understand how important it was that she get a complete physical.

Betina sank her teary face into Maxine's neck. "What's the matter with me?" she whispered. "Why do I feel this way? I hate it, Maxie. I hate it."

"I know, baby," Maxine said with a sniff. "Depression has a way of sneaking up on people, and it seldom goes away on its own."

"What do I have to be depressed about? I've got a wonderful life, a nice home, my own business and a job I love. I make good money, I have a lover who adores me. I don't understand how I could be depressed. It doesn't make any sense."

"It could be something that's been there for years and is just beginning to show itself," Maxine explained. "It could be a chemical imbalance. It could be several things. That's why I want you to see a doctor soon so they can narrow down the problem."

Betina nuzzled her neck. "I really thought I was doing better today."

Maxine hugged her and hoped Betina would keep her word about going to a doctor.

"I got up in time and everything. Joey only had to call me once."

He shouldn't have to call you at all, Maxine thought. Her fear now wasn't so much that Betina's condition wasn't treatable, but that she would continue to be in denial about how serious it was.

"It'll be okay, baby," Maxine said. "When you go see this Dr. Ramirez, make sure you mention that you've been feeling depressed. There are some tests she can give you that'll let her know where you are with that."

Betina sniffed. "Okay, I will."

"And you'll make an appointment tomorrow?"

"I said I would, didn't I?"

Yes, you did, Maxine thought. *That's what you said yesterday and the day before that.*

❧❧

Stuck in afternoon traffic, Maxine kept changing the radio station to see if she could hear what the problem was up ahead. *Maybe Elaine's right about the tourists*, she thought. *Easter is this weekend and every other car seems to be from Mexico.*

When she finally got home, Betina was there but ready to leave again. Pointing to the inside of her arm where a piece of cotton and a Band-Aid were, she said, "I saved the evidence of my doctor's visit today."

Maxine felt a huge sense of relief just knowing that Betina had kept her promise. "So what did she say?"

Betina held her hand up. "No time to talk. I'm meeting Joey at the nursing home for some last minute things for Blue Hair Night. I'll be home late. I picked up Chinese takeout for you. It's in the kitchen. There's a load of laundry on now. I'll pop it in the dryer when I get home."

Maxine shrugged. "I can do that."

"What?" Betina said. She flitted around the room gathering up fashion magazines while trying to put on a shoe. "We're still working on the pizza-in-the-fridge thing, darlin'. You haven't graduated to laundry-in-the-dryer yet."

"Hey, I can do laundry. Who do you think did my laundry in college and med school?"

"Probably one of your girlfriends."

Maxine sensed the underlying meaning in Betina's remarks even though they had been delivered with a smile and an endearing Texas drawl. If taken at face value, the comments were intended to tease, but Maxine knew better. Like a stale cake covered in warm fresh icing, Betina's sarcasm was usually light on the outside, but firm and unappealing once inspected more closely.

"My girlfriends did their own laundry," Maxine said in her own defense.

"Well, I'm off," Betina said, grabbing her purse and keys. "Oh, and I picked up the dry cleaning. Don't wait up for me."

❧❧

Later that night, Maxine felt Betina slip into bed. "Hi, baby," she said as she squinted at the clock. It was a little after midnight. "How did it go?"

"We had fun," Betina said. She put her arm around Maxine's waist and kissed her bare back. "They didn't want us to leave so we stayed until we got everyone done."

"So the dance is tomorrow night?"

"Yes, it's tomorrow night. They want us to go. Even told me to bring my girlfriend." Betina laughed and kissed Maxine's back again.

Once a month Betina and Joey donated several hours to the nursing home close to their salon where they gave haircuts, makeovers, dye-job-touch-ups, perms and washes, sets and curls. There was a dance at the nursing home the last Friday of each month, and it was vitally important that everyone look their best.

"Those old women just *love* Joey," Betina said. "I can't even count the number of times I heard one of them say 'if I was only sixty years younger' while they pinched his cheek."

"Which cheek?" Maxine asked. "The face or the butt?" She was ready to fall back asleep again.

"The face cheeks."

Maxine burrowed deeper into her pillow, but felt a delightfully warm sensation scamper through her body as Betina's fingertip circled Maxine's left nipple.

"I guess you're real sleepy, huh?" Betina said as she kissed Maxine's shoulder and rubbed her breasts against her back.

"Mmm," Maxine murmured, wiggling her butt. "Some things are worth waking up for."

She turned over and kissed her with slow, lazy passion. Maxine's eyes were still closed, but her body was awake and ready for whatever Betina had in mind.

Chapter Fifteen

Maxine saw that she had a message on her cell phone when she got back to her desk in her office. She kept her pager on vibrate and her cell phone off whenever she was with a patient. They deserved her full attention. There was a message from Betina, so she dialed the number to the salon.

"Hair Today," Joey said.

"It's Maxine. Is Betina there?"

"She's with a client, but she can usually trim locks and chat on the phone at the same time. Hold on. Oh, by the way," he said in a hushed tone. "Whatever you said to her has made a huge difference. She's been to work on time two days in a row now and she hasn't been as spacey these past few days."

"She went to the doctor for some tests yesterday," Maxine said, "so hopefully she'll be feeling better soon."

"What? Yesterday? I don't think so," Joey said. "I was with her all day yesterday. She didn't see any doctor."

Momentarily speechless, Maxine eased down on the corner of her desk.

"We closed up the shop late and loaded all the stuff we needed for Blue Hair Night," Joey continued. "Then we stopped for a quick dinner at the Bean Sprout Chinese place down the street. Trust me. She didn't have time to see a doctor yesterday."

Maxine gripped the phone so hard her hand began to hurt. She put the phone against her other ear and got more comfortable on the corner of her desk.

"Maybe she went to the doctor early."

"I woke her up at seven," Joey said.

"What time did she get to work?"

"About eight-thirty. She even picked up breakfast for us, but you know how it usually takes her forever to get ready in the morning. We both got to work early because we started packing things for Blue Hair Night before our first appointments of the day arrived."

"When she got to the shop, did you notice a Band-Aid on her arm?"

"No. Not that I remember."

"Then maybe she went to the doctor after leaving the restaurant yesterday evening."

There was a pause. "Yeah, maybe," Joey said skeptically.

That's probably what happened, she thought. *Betina left the restaurant and went to her appointment after work.*

"Let me talk to her," Maxine said.

"Wait a minute. Did she tell you she went to the doctor yesterday?"

"Let me talk to her."

"Uh-oh. I hear polar cap-sized icicles in your voice. You have to forget whatever stupid thing I just said, Maxie."

"Put her on the phone."

"It's for you," Joey called across the salon, now suddenly very willing to get rid of the phone.

"Take a message," Maxine heard Betina say.

"You better take this one."

"Who is it?"

"Maxie."

"Tell her I'll call her back. I'm busy right now."

"You need to tell her yourself."

"What the—"

Maxine heard grumbling and then the light clickity-click sound of Betina's heels across the tiled floor. Betina picked up the phone and said, "Hi, baby. Can I call you back? I'm in the middle of something."

"I'm returning your call. I have a quick question for you."

"Oh! I have one for you, too. Will you go to the Blue Hair dance with me tonight? We've had three people from the home call here today wanting me and Joey to go. Anyway, think about it and we'll decide later, but it might be fun."

"You *did* go to the doctor yesterday, right?"

There was a pause and then Betina said, "What?"

"The doctor. You went to see the doctor yesterday, right?"

"Why are you asking me that?"

Maxine felt a lump in her throat at just the mere thought of Betina possibly lying to her about this.

"Didn't I tell you I went to the doctor yesterday?"

There was a knock on Maxine's office door and Mona popped her head in. "One in the chute. Exam room three."

"I'll be right there," Maxine said to her.

"I have to go," Betina said.

"So do I. We'll talk about it tonight."

"I'm going to the dance tonight. We can talk there if you decide to go with me."

Betina hung up on her without another word. Maxine closed her cell phone and slipped it back in her lab coat pocket. She stayed there on the corner of her desk until her breathing returned to normal. If Betina lied about a visit to the doctor, Maxine needed to find out why she would do such a thing. *She lives with a doctor,* Maxine thought. *She knows we only want to help people. If she would lie about this, what else is she lying about?* This was all so uncharacteristic of Betina that it had Maxine baffled and unable to explain what was going on in their lives any longer. Suspicion about Betina's motives was now at a premium.

She left her office and walked down the hallway to exam room three. Maxine took the chart out of the plastic holder on the wall by the door and was glad to have work to do and patients to see.

Maxine got home and was greeted by the smell of sautéed onions and Betina puttering around in the kitchen.

"Hi, baby," Betina said. "How was your day?"

"Busy. How was yours?"

"Mine was busy, too. Joey found these cute bunny ears for us to wear. Our clients loved 'em on us. I think Joey likes pretending he's at the Playboy Mansion incognito."

Maxine got a glimpse of the arm Betina had a Band-Aid on the day before and didn't see the traditional bruise where blood had been drawn. Needle sticks usually left a mark on her no matter how good the phlebotomist was. Maxine went directly to their bedroom and into the bathroom they shared. In the small trash can by the vanity Maxine found a Band-Aid wrapper next to a wadded-up tissue. Her heart sank at the realization that Betina more than likely hadn't seen a doctor the day before like she had promised to do.

At dinner Maxine used her doctor's eye as well as a lover's eye to try and find some new insight into Betina's reasoning and behavior. The table at dinner was set with elegant candles, the good china they hadn't used in over a year, ice water, cloth napkins with little Tweety Bird napkin holders, and soft music drifting in from the stereo in the living room. In addition, Betina had prepared a wonderful meal of steak, sautéed onions, mushrooms, and bell pepper, baked potatoes stuffed with cheese and chives, and fresh steamed asparagus. Maxine was aware of the time and care such a meal took to prepare, and she wondered if this change in Betina's behavior had anything to do with her feeling a bit guilty about having lied to her the day before.

"Tell me about your day," Maxine said.

Betina took a sip of water. "Oh, just the usual. Two perms, a few haircuts. Oh! And a purple Chelsea on a sixty-year-old guy who wanted to surprise his new girlfriend. That was a little different."

"Now, a Chelsea is just a lock of hair that's a lot longer than the rest and a different color, right? Am I remembering that correctly?"

Betina laughed. "That's right, darlin'. Very good!"

"Did he say how young his girlfriend was?"

"My age," Betina said. "He was proud of himself for that, too. He had very fine white hair and looked quite distinguished with it. He's an optometrist and has a young customer base, so he wanted to appear more hip with them, too, I guess."

"How did all of that look on him afterward?"

"Ridiculous," Betina said with a chuckle, "but I didn't try and discourage him. After all, I was standing there with bunny ears on probably looking just as ridiculous. But I wouldn't be surprised if he wasn't back in a week or so to have it snipped off."

Maxine had made up her mind to call Joey the next day and ask him some questions about how Betina was functioning during the day. Things weren't adding up or making sense to her. She needed more information than she could get on her own, and Joey was the best resource she had.

"So will you be my date for the Blue Hair dance tonight?" Betina asked.

Surprised by the question, Maxine's eyes widened. "If you're serious about going, then of course I will."

"Then we can leave right after dinner. It won't last too long," Betina said. "I don't think older people stay up very late."

"Why shouldn't they? I bet they might surprise you."

115

"We've been getting so many requests to block off the last Friday of the month just for them," Betina said. "They all want their hair done the day *of* the dance. Not the day before, but since we're volunteering our time and everything, that's not feasible for us. So as it stands now, some of the women tend to sleep sitting up on Thursday night so as not to mess up their hair." She fluffed up her baked potato with her fork. "Those old men don't have to worry about things like that, though. Most of them don't have any hair."

"These seniors might still surprise you."

Betina smiled at her. "Maybe."

Maxine was happy to see Betina's excitement about going to the dance. On their way out the door after dinner, Betina told her to bring a stack of business cards.

"I'll post one for you on the bulletin board and leave some at the front desk. Joey and I get a lot of business from relatives who visit there."

As Maxine got in the car, she was even more amazed when she realized how quickly Betina had gotten dressed for the dance. There had been no primping or fretting over what dress would be best or what shoes would match. Maxine remembered her first experience with Betina and shoes. They had only known each other a short time when Betina sent her to the car to get a pair of "tall shoes" from the trunk.

"Tall shoes. What color are they?" Maxine asked.

"Black."

"And what exactly are 'tall shoes' anyway?"

"You know," Betina said. "Tall shoes. With a higher heel than the ones I have on now. Tall shoes."

"Okay. No problem."

So with unfounded confidence, Maxine left her condo with Betina's car keys in search for "tall shoes" in the trunk of her car. She got to Betina's car, opened the trunk and was shocked at what she saw. There had to have been thirty pairs of black shoes, and twenty-five of them looked exactly alike to her. Most were lined up in an orderly fashion—some still in boxes.

"Oh," Maxine said. "The tall *black* ones."

There were sandals, boots, loafers, slides, low heels, medium heels, high heels, come-fuck-me pumps, and other shoe types that Maxine couldn't even begin to describe or name.

"The black tall ones," she mumbled while shuffling through the pile. Maxine found two that matched with what she thought would be considered a "tall" heel and closed the trunk. When she got back to her condo, she held the shoes up and said, "Did I get the right ones?"

"Yes, baby. Perfect."

"Whew," Maxine said, letting out a deep breath. "I feel like I passed some sort of test or something. Why do you have all your shoes in the trunk of your car?"

The incredulous look Betina gave her made Maxine stop and examine the question she had just asked, but she couldn't find anything wrong with what she had said.

"*All* of my shoes?" Betina said. "Those are just the ones that won't fit in my closet at home, darlin'. That's the overflow." She shook her head. "All my shoes. Just wait until you *see* all of my shoes!"

That entire "tall shoes" experience had been a real eye-opener for Maxine. She had been with several feminine women before, but never one with so many accessories or such an interesting sense of fashion. According to Betina, her explanation for such feminine qualities stemmed from having a gay brother.

"Something happened to us in the womb. He liked my placenta better, but I wouldn't give it up until I was finished with it."

Betina believed that since she and Joey were twins, it gave them an even stronger bond than most siblings.

"You can't share a womb with someone for nine months and not be close. Once you're womb-mates with someone, it doesn't just end there, you know."

Betina was also quick to mention that she and Joey had to come out of the closet at an early age because they needed the room for more shoes.

So when Betina was ready for the dance *and* had prepared an elaborate meal after work, Maxine was left wondering again what had happened to the Betina she knew. Other than the First Wednesday Night gatherings and going to dinner together after a long day, they seldom went out anywhere after work and now here they were going to a dance. It was unusual and somewhat spontaneous for them, and Maxine liked the idea of spending more time with Betina this way.

As she drove to the dance, Maxine glanced over at her and felt relieved to see her lover primping in the mirror on the visor and touching up her lipstick. *That's more like it*, she thought with relief. *I've missed all that foo-fooing she usually does.*

Chapter Sixteen

Maxine smiled as she watched Betina pin a business card on the bulletin board in the main hallway of the nursing home and then place a small stack of them at the front desk alongside others that were already there. It warmed her heart to be there with her, and Maxine adored her for the type of volunteer work Betina and her brother did for those who could no longer go to them for their services. She met Betina halfway and Maxine could hear Jerry Lee Lewis's "Great Balls of Fire" coming from somewhere in the facility. She offered her arm to escort Betina to the dance.

"Here," Betina said, sticking a few business cards in Maxine's shirt pocket. "Now you'll have some of mine and yours in case anyone asks you who did the hair for this event." Giving Maxine's arm a pat, she said, "And you just never know who'll eventually be needing a pap when we're out somewhere either. Just don't get those cards mixed up, baby." She threw her head back and laughed. "Can you imagine that? Someone asking about Ms. So-And-So's hair and then you hand them *your* business card instead of mine?"

"I'm almost positive I won't be handing out any business cards this evening. I'm here to have fun."

"Oh, you never know."

Every now and then Betina took a shot at designing a business card encompassing both their professions, but she could never come up with anything either of them liked. While perusing a draft of a potential card Betina had done, Maxine once told her, "Not many patients feel like getting their hair done when they come to see me, you know."

"The new cards won't be suggesting our services be used at the same *time*, for goodness sakes!"

"I can see it now," Maxine said. "Hair Today slash Pelvic Exams. I don't even want to *think* about the logo for such a thing."

"Yeah, yeah, yeah," Betina would always say as she tossed away yet another draft. "I know. I know. Bad idea. But it would only give them one card to keep up with for us."

When they finally arrived at the cafeteria down at the end of the hall, Maxine immediately noticed the colorful decorations. Taped to the walls were inflatable guitars in an array of pastel colors, and there were huge music notes hanging from the ceiling that came to life each time the central air unit came on. There were posters of Elvis and Little Richard hanging behind the DJ, who had an elaborate setup of portable stereo equipment. A man in his late seventies, the DJ repositioned a speaker and looked old enough to live there at the facility, but could just as easily have been another volunteer for the event.

"You think any of these people know there's newer music out there now?" Betina whispered.

"I'm sure they do."

"Will you look at that?" Betina exclaimed.

Across the room in the direction Betina pointed, Maxine saw Joey waving at them. He was talking to three women and waved them over. One of the women had to be in her eighties and stood with the aid of a walker, while the other two—a blonde and a brunette—were closer to Maxine and Betina's ages.

"He's giving up a Friday night at the bar for Blue Hair Night?" Maxine whispered. "What a nice thing to do!"

"Are you kidding?" Betina said. "Only a geek would go to the bar before eleven. Plus, there's free food here, not to mention he's probably passed out a whole box of business cards by now! Not only is he *here*, but he's here *early!*"

She let go of Maxine's arm as they approached Joey and the women on the other side of the room. Once they got closer, Maxine noticed that Joey had a button on his shirt that said: Tease that hair up to Jesus!

There were chairs along the walls where several of the residents were sitting and chatting. No one was dancing yet, but there was definitely some finger-wagging and shoulder dipping to the beat of the music.

"Betina!" the older woman exclaimed. "Come here and meet my lesbian daughter and her partner."

"Mrs. Davenport!" Betina said. "Your hair looks fabulous! Who does it for you?"

Everyone in the immediate area laughed.

"You should hear what your brother's been telling us," Mrs. Davenport said. "What a little scoundrel he is."

"Which one of you is Betina?" the blonde next to Joey asked. Her rich Texas accent made Maxine smile. It was a little more pronounced than Betina's, but just as sexy and endearing.

"I'm Betina. Which one of you is the lesbian daughter and which one is the lesbian daughter's partner?"

"Mavis Davis," the blonde said, introducing herself. "I'm the lesbian daughter's partner. Mrs. D can't stop talkin' about the nice work you and your brother do here."

"Laura Davenport," the brunette said as she shook Betina's hand. "I'm the lesbian daughter. My mother's told me so much about you."

121

Mavis Davis, Maxine thought. *Would someone really name a child something like that on purpose?*

"And this is my partner, Dr. Maxine Weston," Betina said proudly.

Maxine smiled at the three women and couldn't help but be amused by Betina's use of her "doctor" title when introducing her. Maxine seldom used it in this type of setting, but last names were flying around all over the place here for some reason.

"Dr. Maxine Weston?" Mavis said. "The lesbian-gynecologist-Doctor-Maxine-Weston?"

Betina's delighted laughter was infectious, making Joey and the others in the group laugh, too. "One and the same," Betina said.

Mavis looked right at Maxine and said, "It's almost impossible to get an appointment with you."

"I've heard that before," Maxine replied apologetically. "All I can do is recommend you keep trying. I have cancellations all the time. My partner's also a good—"

"But he's a guy, right?"

"Yes."

"Well, you know what they say about male gynecologists," Mavis said.

"Hey, I'm *outta* this conversation!" Joey said in mock horror.

"What's wrong with a male gynecologist?" Mrs. Davenport asked.

"Let's just say you probably wouldn't take your dog to a veterinarian who didn't have any pets, would you?"

"My dog?" Mrs. Davenport said. "I don't have a dog anymore."

"Oh, I see," Laura said. "That's like the concept of 'don't take your car to a mechanic who doesn't drive,' right?"

"Exactly, darlin'," Mavis said.

"I don't have a car either," Mrs. Davenport said. "My daughter thinks I'm too old to drive."

"It's a requirement that you be able to see over the steering wheel, Mother."

122

Betina's laughter set them all off again.

"So what was the question?" Mrs. Davenport asked.

"Oh, never mind," Mavis said.

"Do you have a business card or something?" Laura asked Maxine. "Even if I have to wait six months or so for an appointment, I'd much rather see a female gynecologist."

Betina regained her composure long enough to reach into Maxine's shirt pocket and pull out four business cards, giving two each to the younger women.

"In case you need your hair done before your appointment with my lesbian gynecologist girlfriend here."

Betina and Joey got the dancing started to "Johnny B. Goode" and after several minutes of swinging each other around the dance floor like teenage bobby soxers, they went out into the crowd and selected two of the elderly residents to dance with. Before long it seemed as though everyone was dancing—some with canes and walkers, and a few even in wheelchairs. After a vigorous whirl of "Rock Around the Clock" finished playing, Joey and Betina came back to the refreshment table where Maxine was standing. Next to the punch bowl were several platters of cookies in the shape of Easter eggs and and pastel-colored cupcakes with Easter jelly beans stuck on top. The three of them continued to watch the dancers and sip punch. Maxine spotted Laura and Mavis dancing around Mrs. Davenport and her walker several feet away from them. A few minutes later a little old man with a cane came over and asked Betina to dance.

"Nice haircut, Mr. Lopez!" Maxine heard Betina say as she led him out on the dance floor.

Helping himself to another cup of punch, Joey announced, "Well, I'm gonna blow this popcorn stand."

"Do you have a minute?" Maxine asked him.

"Sure. What's up?"

"Let's go some place where we can talk."

She led the way out through the cafeteria door and into the hallway. They found an elderly couple talking and standing close enough together to be having a serious conversation. They became flustered and scurried back inside, causing the metal cafeteria door to close behind them with a hearty clunk.

"So what's the matter?" Joey asked. Maxine heard the concern in his voice and could see it in his pale blue eyes.

"As long as I've known Betina," Maxine started, "she's never really been sick. Nothing more than a cold and nothing that would warrant her having to see a doctor."

"You mean a doctor other than Dr. Abernathy?"

"Dr. Abernathy," Maxine said. "Yes. The retired pediatrician."

Joey laughed. "Don't say it like that! He's taken care of us for years. Our whole lives even."

"Don't tell me he's the only physician *you* have!"

Joey shrugged. "I haven't been sick since he retired."

"Well, get another doctor! I don't believe you two. You're both over thirty. What's the matter with you?"

"Okay, okay. Chill, Maxie. What's the matter? What's gotten you so riled up?"

Suddenly, Maxine was unsure about what to do next or how much to tell him. Letting Joey know that Betina had lied about seeing a doctor didn't seem wise at the moment. It was personal information and none of his concern. What Maxine really wanted from him was information about Betina's relationship with her old doctor. Things just weren't adding up.

"Betina seems unwilling to see a physician now," she said. "I was hoping you could shed some light on why that would be such a problem for her."

Joey took a sip of his punch. "She lives with one. Wouldn't that be enough?"

"What's that supposed to mean?"

Joey shrugged. "Why should she be out the expense and inconvenience of going to see a doctor when she *lives* with one? That's what I mean."

"I'm not her doctor."

"Then I can't answer your question. I don't know why she doesn't want to go."

"You're not helping me."

"I *do* know she doesn't like shrinks," Joey said. "Our parents had a hard time getting her to see one."

Maxine's eyes widened and she felt as though someone had thumped her on the forehead. "Wait, wait, wait," she managed to say. "Betina's been treated by a psychiatrist before?"

"Sure. We both were," he said matter-of-factly.

"Holy moly."

Chapter Seventeen

Maxine didn't know what to say. She stood there blinking as her mind raced to retrieve some previously stored information, but nothing was coming to her. It did occur to her, however, that there were obviously huge gaps in Betina's life that she knew nothing about. That in itself was almost as unsettling as the knowledge that Betina had lied to her about going to the doctor.

"You and Betina have been treated by a psychiatrist in the past?"

Joey looked away from her. "I don't want to talk about any of this, Maxie."

"It's way too late for that, buddy. How old were you when this happened?"

"You'll have to ask Betina."

"No," Maxine said. "I'm asking you."

He seemed to panic for a moment and took a few steps back away from her. "It's not something I'm proud of, okay? This whole thing stood between us for years."

"All the more reason for you to tell me about it now, Joey. I think Betina needs us. This is very important."

Maxine took a deep breath. *And it's so unethical for me to be doing this!* she thought. *Prying into someone's medical history . . . Hippocrates will probably strike you dead right where you stand, Dr. Weston.*

"It was a long time ago," Joey said. "We were just kids."

Lowering her voice in hopes of relaying the empathy she felt as well as wanting to coax answers from him, Maxine said, "Tell me what happened. All kids do things they aren't proud of. That's part of growing up. It's how we learn."

He glanced at his watch and then shook his head. "Maybe we can do this some other time. I've got people to do and things to see this evening."

"You're not leaving until we talk."

"I can't do this now. I'm meeting some friends at the bar."

"Only a geek goes to the bar before eleven," Maxine reminded him, borrowing a quote from Betina. "It's only eight-thirty. Now start talking."

There was a sitting area around the corner from the cafeteria. Joey started walking that way and plopped down in one of the over-stuffed chairs. Maxine sat in the one across from him. She vaguely noticed the Easter decorations hanging from the ceiling. The music filtering out from the cafeteria was less intrusive where they were now, but "Jail House Rock" could still be heard from down the hall-way.

"How old were you when this happened?" Maxine asked.

"We were fourteen," he said while crossing his legs and focusing on his right shoe. "It all started with a lie . . . well . . . yeah, it was a lie . . . I lied about something and—"

Maxine waited for him to continue, but she could see how troubled he was. If he bolted now, there was no telling when she would get another opportunity like this one.

Finally, he said, "I'll start at the beginning." He uncrossed his legs and leaned forward in the chair. "My mother was cleaning my room one day and found some . . . magazines."

She waited a moment and decided to let him do this his way. On the outside Maxine was calm and attentive, but on the inside she wanted to shake him to get to the story faster.

"These were not the type of magazines most fourteen-year-old boys hide in their rooms," he said in a low monotone as he focused on his shoes again. "They were gay porn magazines. Hard core stuff. Raunchy . . . big . . . well . . . you get the picture."

Wow, Maxine thought. *That scene couldn't have been pleasant for his mother*. She had never met Betina's and Joey's parents, but what little she had heard about them hadn't impressed her much. They lived in Hawaii now and visits to Texas were rare. Betina and Joey hadn't seen them in several years. The one time Maxine tried to get any information about why they were estranged, Betina refused to talk about it.

"Then what happened?" Maxine asked.

Joey cleared his throat. "My mother was there waiting for me when I got home from school. Even now when I think about it, my knees start knocking together." His embarrassed laugh didn't hide the uneasiness in his eyes. He laced his fingers together to keep his hands from trembling.

"What did she say to you?"

Joey shook his head. "Some of it I've blocked out of my mind, but I do remember her standing at the bottom of the stairs waving the magazines in my face. I was paralyzed and afraid. Humiliated and ashamed. I thought my life was over, Maxie."

"What did you do?"

"I did the only thing I *could* do at the time," he said. He leaned back in the chair and crossed his arms over his chest. "I told my mother the magazines were Betina's."

Maxine looked at him to see if he was serious, and when she saw his eyes mist over with tears, she slumped back in her chair.

"Oh, no."

"Oh, yes," he said. "I saved my little faggot ass and blamed the whole thing on her." He brushed away more tears with the back of his hand. "Betina came home from cheerleading practice later that afternoon. My mother had called my dad out of a business meeting to help her handle the situation. She was hysterical. I can't even begin to tell you how scared I was. When my dad arrived home, he was already pissed. The three of us were waiting for Betina when she got there. When she finally walked into the house, she was met by our parents waving the filthy magazines in her face and me peeking around behind them mouthing 'I'm sorry!' over and over again." He stopped long enough to run his fingers through his thick blond hair. "Just the thought of my mother seeing those magazines . . . ohmigod. I'm surprised I was ever able to get it up again." He sniffed and cleared his throat. "So now instead of having what they initially thought was a gay son, my parents now think they have a tramp for a daughter. I mean think about it, Maxie. Those pictures were one thing for some old gay geezer to have, but for me to insinuate they were Betina's . . . well . . . any fourteen-year-old girl who would have copies of *Big Dicks R Us* would appear to have more than a few problems!"

"Insinuate?" Maxine repeated. "You didn't *insinuate* anything, Joey." Her heart went out to Betina. All she wanted to do right then was find her and hold her. Finally, Maxine asked, "What did Betina have to say in her defense?"

"Nothing."

"Nothing?"

"Nothing," Joey said, exhausted. "Zip. She didn't deny or acknowledge anything, and she and I didn't speak for two years after that no matter how many times I tried to apologize or thank her for helping me. Our parents pulled her out of all school activities and put her on restriction for six months. To and from school. That's all she could do. No TV. No stereo. No phone calls. No cheerleading. No nothing. To and from school. Period. And to get even with us, Betina refused to speak to anyone when she was home. After the first two weeks of the silent treatment, they got a little worried about her and sent her to a psychiatrist. Betina hated going and refused to talk to the shrink either. The only good thing to come out of all that was the way our parents thought they would get even with her for not talking anymore. They were still pretty freaked out about everything. They eventually put her in one of those all girls' Catholic schools here in town. To them it seemed like the perfect place for her at the time . . . no boys . . . nice religious setting . . . nuns who were serious about academics. But what they didn't count on was all the little Catholic lesbians that were there. Betina was in high school heaven once she got settled in."

They shared a light chuckle over that.

"So Betina kept your secret?" Maxine asked.

"She did, and she paid a high price for it. I know for a fact that if our positions had been reversed, I would've spilled my guts to save myself. It's one of those character flaws I have, and just one more thing I'm not proud of. I liked being gay, but I didn't want anyone to know about it."

"When did your parents find out about you?"

"I finally came out when they insisted I go to college," Joey said. "I told them I wanted to be a hairdresser. That didn't go over very well." He offered a sad smile. "Me being gay was a no-brainer for them after that. A while later, they also realized who the magazines had really belonged to after all. Unfortunately, Betina was also out by then, so there was no way my parents were going to make up for what all happened. In their eyes, being a lesbian was much worse than having porn magazines in one's possession. And once Betina came out to them, our parents were suddenly wishing those magazines *had* belonged to her." He shrugged. "But in their eyes, Betina's interest in vaginas still wasn't as bad as their son liking big dicks." His statement was uttered with humor, but she could still see the pain and shame in his eyes. Maxine realized that Joey hadn't come to terms with his lifestyle nor his parents' rejection. It was a personal journey each gay or lesbian person must take, and on their own terms.

More or less thinking out loud, Maxine said, "So if Betina wasn't talking to you during those early days, then there's no real way of knowing what went on between her and the psychiatrist."

"She talked about it a little a few years ago," Joey said. "It's not a subject we dwell on much. According to her, she would go to the shrink's office and stare out the window for an hour while he caught up on notes from his other patients. Betina didn't speak to him and he didn't really report that back to anyone. My parents thought the sessions were helping her, when in fact, nothing at all was going on or getting accomplished."

"I see." *This doesn't sound good*, Maxine thought. *I might have a hard time convincing her to try therapy again.*

"Betina gave us all a scare another time, too," he said. "We thought she had taken up drinking and sneaking booze from my dad's liquor cabinet. She was about sixteen then, I guess . . . before she came out. For them at the time, it just seemed to reinforce the theory that she was wild and boy-crazy. After all, nice girls don't get drunk and look at dirty magazines."

Still having a bit of trouble accepting Joey's betrayal, Maxine tried to focus more on why she was there—she needed more answers.

"Was Betina ever treated for depression?"

"With that loser of a shrink she had? I'm sure she was never treated for anything."

"How long did the drinking last?"

"A few months before she got caught."

"Have you known her to abuse alcohol at any time since then?" Maxine asked. "Any binge drinking? Betina isn't much of a drinker now. At least she hasn't been during the time I've known her."

"She drank more when she was with Cory. Betina wasn't happy in that relationship."

Cory Catalani, Maxine thought. *The photographer who was low on talent and high on ego. Those two were a very bad match from the beginning.*

"You mentioned that both of you saw a psychiatrist," Maxine said. "When and why did your parents send you to see one?"

131

"Like I said, Betina and I weren't speaking. I was too afraid she would squeal on me about the magazines, so I just stayed out of her way. But meals around the house were *not* pleasant. Before the magazine incident, dinner time with the Abbotts was a family thing where we were expected to discuss current events and national and city politics. Almost like a pop quiz with food, only Betina wasn't talking anymore. That made me not want to talk either. It just seemed like a good idea for me to keep my mouth shut. I was in constant fear of Betina outing me. I knew I deserved it, so like I said, I stayed out of her way. I didn't want to take the chance of provoking her, so I didn't say much at home either. Finally my father got tired of it and sent me off to a shrink, too. It didn't last long since I can fake almost anything. I straightened my young gay ass up for an hour a week until it was officially announced I was okay."

"Is that everything?"

"That's the way I remember it," he said. "I'm not sure you'll be able to get her back to a shrink, though. She's got some bad memories of all that. I hear that forced therapy never works, and she shouldn't have been in therapy anyway. The whole thing was just all fucked up, Maxie. I think what really sent her spiraling downward was some of the things my mother said to her. My parents got her alone and called her some names that upset her to this day. She hasn't been able to talk to me about it yet. Even after all this time."

"At least now I know what I'm up against. I appreciate your candor."

Joey stood up. "Betina's lucky to have you."

Maxine got up, too, and gave him a hug. "Actually, I'm the lucky one."

Maxine went back to the cafeteria and found almost everyone up and dancing to "Blue Moon." Laura Davenport and her mother were by the refreshment table, with Mrs. Davenport hanging on to her walker, but still swaying to the music. Across the room Maxine could see Betina dancing with the DJ, while Mavis Davis danced with two women in wheelchairs. Before she knew what was happening, Maxine found herself dancing with the older couple she had seen in the hallway earlier. Each took one of her hands and attempted to give her a twirl, only to find themselves in a tangle of arms. By the time the song ended, there was a collective, "Whew!" from the crowd as everyone headed for the punch bowl.

"There you are!" Betina said. She came up behind Maxine and briefly put her hands on her waist. "Where were you? None of these old men believe I'm here with my girlfriend."

"I was talking to Joey."

"Where is that pink flamingo on the great lawn of life anyway? Did he leave already?"

"According to him, he was going to the bar," Maxine said. "He must be feeling like a geek tonight or something."

She noticed that the line at the refreshment table got much shorter once "Sixteen Candles" began to play and everyone made their way to the dance floor. Many couples began to sway to the music while others danced in groups of three or more. Several of the older residents sat down and fanned themselves instead, choosing to watch for a while.

"Let's take some punch around," Betina suggested. "They can't very well use a walker and carry a cup at the same time."

Maxine helped Betina fill some cups with punch and then put them on a tray. After a while they had a system worked out where Maxine filled the cups and Betina and Mavis took them to those who couldn't fend for themselves. As Maxine watched her lover talk to the residents and compliment them on their hair, she couldn't help but feel that familiar tugging at her heart.

Chapter Eighteen

On the way home, Betina was animated and chatty. She seemed more like her old self and it made Maxine leery about bringing up unpleasant subjects. She had spent the latter part of the evening processing everything Joey had told her. The most remarkable piece of information for her had been the way Betina had taken the blame for having the magazines and how she had protected her brother from the humiliation that was sure to have followed. It was an act of courage and spunk for someone so young. Maxine still saw those characteristics in the Betina she knew. She also found it interesting that Betina would make her brother pay for the lie by not speaking to him for years. The incident with Joey and the magazine obviously triggered Betina's initial bouts of depression when she was a teenager, but that didn't explain why she would now feel the need to lie about seeing a doctor for a checkup. Maxine felt as though she had waited long enough and had been able to separate herself from her initial disappointment at having been lied to. It was time to approach the subject and get it behind them.

"Did you have fun tonight?" Betina asked. She turned on the radio and found a jazz station.

"I did. And you were right about the business cards," Maxine said. "I think I might have picked up two new patients this evening."

"That Mavis Davis person is a real character," Betina said. "Some old guy wanted to dance with her and by the time she finished swinging him around, his toupee had flown off and his tie was on backward. He loved it! Made her promise to dance with him again." She threw her head back and cackled. "After that I thought he was heading for the punch bowl, but Mavis said he was more than likely looking for the med cart. She worked him over pretty good."

Maxine pulled into their driveway and then into the garage, and the motion detector light popped on. She turned the ignition off and sat there for a moment, wanting to say everything that was running through her head, but not sure where to start.

"Are you tired, baby?" Betina asked.

"A little."

"Thank you for going to Blue Hair Night with me."

"Well, thanks for asking me."

Betina reached for her hand. "I'm not looking forward to getting old."

"I don't think anyone does."

"Most of it's not pretty." Betina leaned her head back then turned to look at Maxine. "Why are we still in the car?"

Maxine chuckled. "I don't know. Other than the fact it's comfortable in here. You ready to go in?"

They got out of the car and went in the house through the kitchen entrance. It was dark inside, but felt nice and cool. Maxine decided that she couldn't put things off any longer. She took Betina by the hand and led the way to the sofa in the living room.

"Let's sit for a few minutes," Maxine suggested. "I have something to ask you."

Betina sat down and slipped off her shoes. Maxine sat beside her and took a deep breath.

"What am I going to do with you?" Maxine asked quietly.

"You could rub my feet with some of that lotion, for starters," Betina said. She turned and put her bare feet up in Maxine's lap. Maxine reached for a tube of lotion on the coffee table and began rubbing it in between Betina's toes.

"I know you didn't go to the doctor this week like you told me you would," Maxine said. "First of all, I want you to know I'm not angry about that anymore. I might be a little confused about your reasons for wanting to deceive me, but I'm not upset about it."

Maxine could feel Betina's legs stiffen and her feet were suddenly flexed. Maxine made it a point to keep her voice calm and her tone low and sympathetic.

"I just have a few questions to ask you."

"I think I'm ready for bed now," Betina said as she attempted to sit up.

Maxine held her legs in her lap and prevented her from moving.

"Just give me a few minutes," Maxine said.

"I can't talk about this."

"Sure you can, baby. It's me. The woman who loves you more than anything. Whatever the problem is, we'll deal with it together."

"There isn't a problem," Betina said. "I'm getting up on time, I'm paying the bills now, I'm—"

"This isn't about any of that, Betina. We've been over this already. My questions have to do with your inability and unwillingness to have your health evaluated by a professional. You seem to have this intense dislike for doctors and I'd like to know where it's coming from."

Betina's body was still tense, but she was no longer attempting to get up and leave.

"I can't explain any of that to you."

"Let's give it a try anyway," Maxine said. She continued working the lotion into Betina's toes and then moved to the heel of her right foot. "Is it the doctor's office? The waiting room? Needles for lab work? What in particular is causing all of this?"

"I don't know," Betina said in a small voice.

"Or could it be that you're afraid of what the doctor might find during an examination?"

"Yeah," she replied in the same tiny voice. "Maybe that."

"I can arrange to go with you."

"No!" Betina said. She jerked her foot away, but Maxine put it back in her lap.

"Or I can arrange to stay completely out of it."

"Why can't you see that I'm doing better?" Betina asked with a sniff.

We've had this conversation before already, Maxine thought. She took another slow, deep breath and kept working the lotion in.

"You'll just have to trust me on this one, baby," Maxine said. "If you're afraid of what the doctor will say, all I can do is remind you that you aren't alone. We'll handle it together. But first you have to give the tests a chance and let a professional do what they're trained to do."

"And what if they find something wrong?" Betina asked. Her voice broke and tears rolled down her cheeks. "I mean *really* wrong? What if I'm nuts like my mother? What if they find out I *am* depressed and I have to see a shrink?" She swung her legs around and got her feet on the floor. "I'm not seeing another one, Maxie. I'm not wasting my time and my money on any of that nonsense."

Maxine put the cap back on the tube of lotion and set it on the coffee table.

"You mentioned your mother being nuts," Maxine said. "What exactly did you mean by that?"

"Oh, no you don't," Betina said. "I'm not talking about this."

"Yes, you are. I want to know what's going on with you. I *deserve* to know that. Our lives are in chaos right now and you're unwilling to do anything about it."

"I'm going to bed," Betina said, and stormed out of the room.

Maxine sat there on the sofa and tried to figure out a way to get Betina through this "doctor phobia" she seemed to have. *If I've got to play hardball, then so be it*, she thought.

When Maxine entered their bedroom, she found Betina sitting on her side of the bed crying. Maxine went to her and put her arm around her waist. Seeing Betina cry made Maxine cry, too.

Finally, Maxine kissed the top of Betina's head and said, "It's okay, baby. We'll figure this out together."

Betina buried her tear-stained face in Maxine's neck and whispered, "I'm sorry I lied to you about going to see the doctor." She sniffed and wiped her eyes with the back of her hand. "Was it that damned Barbie Band-Aid that gave me away?"

Maxine laughed and dabbed at her own tears. "No. You flashed your arm so quickly I didn't get a chance to see the Band-Aid. Joey told me he'd been with you all day and there's no way you'd had time to see a doctor."

"Joey's got the biggest flappin' lips I've—"

"Don't blame him," Maxine said. "Please. He's being very helpful with all of this."

"How? By ratting on me?"

"No. By giving me answers that I can't seem to get from you."

"Anything you want to know, just ask me."

All Maxine had to do was give her a squinty look.

Betina nodded. "Yeah, yeah, yeah. I know. But you keep asking hard things that I don't want to get into."

They shared a small laugh together.

"Well, time's running out, my love," Maxine said. "You got busted on the Barbie Band-Aid and you still haven't seen a doctor. I need you to tell me what it's going to take to get you there. Do Joey and I have to load you up in the car and take you kicking and screaming? Should I have a friend make a house call? Do I need to buy you something outrageously expensive and use it like a little bribe?"

Betina lay back on the bed and propped herself up with a pillow. "How expensive is *outrageously* expensive?"

Maxine looked at her and recognized that gleam in her eye. *You finally have her attention*, she thought and then shrugged. "I don't know. Jewelry? An exotic vacation? A new car? What would it take?"

Betina reached for the buttons on Maxine's shirt. "Hmm. Let me think about it." She urged her closer so their lips were barely touching. "I never realized how much I enjoyed being bribed before. I think I really *really* like it."

"Money is no object if it gets you to the doctor."

Betina pulled Maxine down on top of her, then wrapped her long, shapely legs around her back. "Hmm. Money is no object. I think I like the sound of that, too."

Chapter Nineteen

Their lovemaking was hot and passionate, and Maxine felt closer to Betina than she'd felt in weeks. With their clothes strewn about the room and only the light from the bathroom to guide them, Maxine enjoyed being nestled between Betina's legs, feasting on her. The moment her tongue touched Betina's quivering flesh, Maxine knew there would be a reason to celebrate later.

"Guess what?" she said as she rubbed the end of her nose against Betina's swollen clitoris.

"Is she out?" Betina gasped. "Is she?"

"About the size of a peanut so far."

"Ohmigod," Betina said, and filled her hands with Maxine's hair. "Just keep licking, baby. Show her how happy we are to see her again."

Maxine knew that when Betina's clitoris was this big so early during their lovemaking, "she" would grow even bigger as the stimulation continued. Maxine needed to remember the different sizes it would eventually become so she could compare them to something more easily envisioned, like a nut or a piece of candy. The more creative Maxine could be with her descriptions, the better Betina liked it. They would usually spend several hours over the next few days discussing "her" size and the length of "her" stay. Betina absolutely lived for the nights when "she" was out and presenting "herself." After a round of thrashing, bumping, and humping, Betina pulled Maxine up, cuddled her in her arms and wanted a thorough narration of how things had progressed "down there" since "she" had appeared.

"She was *out!*" Betina squealed. "Ohmigod! It's been *ages!*"

Maxine hugged her and couldn't help but get caught up in Betina's excitement.

"How long has it been?"

"About six months, I guess," Maxine said.

"What can I do for you, baby?" Betina asked, kissing her on the lips.

"I'm fine. I came when you did."

"Really? Let me see." Betina reached down and slipped her fingers into Maxine. "Ohhh. Yes, baby. So you did."

They spent another ten minutes or so going over the remarkable "clit sighting" that had taken place. Betina couldn't hear enough about it and continued on with a string of questions.

"So how big do you think she was?"

"Hmm. Maybe the size of a plump peanut."

"Or maybe a small walnut?"

Maxine laughed. She loved the way Betina tried to make her clitoris sound even bigger no matter what Maxine tried to compare it to.

"No. Not that big," Maxine said. "More like the size of a jaw breaker, maybe."

Betina caressed Maxine's cheek with such tenderness that it made her heart skip a beat. "A big jaw breaker or a little jaw breaker?"

Maxine chuckled and realized she needed to brush up on the names of some hard candy.

"So it was good?" Maxine finally asked.

"I can't remember the last time I had one like that. It was fabulous."

She kissed Betina on the forehead. "We'll check her out again in the morning."

"She never shows herself two days in a row," Betina said with a pout. "It's kind of like late Christmas Day when you're a kid. You've gotta wait a whole year for Christmas morning to come around again."

"It's never taken her a year to show up," Maxine said sleepily. "Maybe she'll surprise us in the morning."

After a moment, Betina said, "I want to thank you for not making such a big deal about the Barbie Band-Aid thing. I don't know what I was thinking. Eventually you would've asked about the test results. I'm usually more with-it than that."

"Just remember that you're not alone with this, okay? I'm here and I'll help you."

"Maybe it's time I tell you what I've been up to then."

Maxine was suddenly very awake. Whatever relaxing effect her orgasm had given her earlier had now been zapped from her entire body.

"Yes," Maxine said. "Maybe you should tell me what you've been up to."

Betina sat up in bed and switched on the light on her nightstand. She opened the drawer and pulled out a thin book—a catalog of herbs, biochemic cell salts, and other homeopathic products.

"I started reading up on this," Betina said shyly. "There's a little test in the booklet that you can take and then it has the herbs that help with the symptoms a person's been having."

Maxine took the pamphlet from her and scanned the pages Betina had marked. "So have you been reading up on herbs? Or have you been taking them?" she asked.

"I read first," Betina admitted, "but I've been taking some recently."

"How recently?"

"For about a week now."

Maxine could feel a flicker of anger coming to life inside of her. Betina leaned over and got something else out of the drawer on the nightstand. She brought back a bottle of St. John's Wort and another dark bottle about the same size.

"Where did you get this one?" Maxine asked, holding up the bottle with "W#174" printed on the label.

"Page fourteen. I ordered it after I took the test I mentioned. It's helped me a lot. I'm feeling much better now."

Maxine turned to page fourteen and read about "Nerve Wise's #174" in the center of the page. This particular bottle contained cimicifuga, gelsemium, ignatia, and kali phos. The keynotes next to the picture in the catalog suggested these items were good for anxiety, insomnia, tension, and cramps.

"You'll need to let your new doctor know about these when you go to your appointment," Maxine said in an even voice. She was so proud of herself for staying calm and level-headed.

"You're not mad?"

"What good would that do?" Maxine set the bottles and the pamphlet on her nightstand on her side of the bed—as far away from Betina as she could possibly get them at the moment.

"I expected you to be all . . . all . . ."

"All what?"

"All pissed off about this."

"And what good would that do, I ask again?" Maxine laid back down. "Turn off the light and come here."

Betina did as she was told. "You're scaring me," she said with a nervous laugh. "Why aren't you upset?"

"At this point, I'm just glad you're talking about it. I don't want to do anything or say anything that'll make you feel as though I don't understand what you're going through." Maxine hugged her and kissed the top of her head. "This is me being supportive."

"Well, I guess I'm not used to that. Hey, I know how you feel about herbal medicine and all that witch doctor stuff."

"But you went ahead and ordered something and kept it hidden from me anyway."

Betina sank deeper into her arms. "It seemed like a good idea at the time."

"I know," Maxine whispered. She tucked her anger and frustration away long enough to realize how important it was that Betina had shared this with her. "All I have to say on this subject is that herbs have had their place in medical history," Maxine said, "but we've progressed beyond what they can do for us now. There are a number of medications that can change things for the better. I would prefer that we find out what the problem is and treat it that way."

"I know," Betina said quietly. "That's the speech I was waiting for, only I expected it to be a lot louder."

"Well, if it helps, I'm yelling on the inside."

Maxine continued to hold her and could feel Betina's sweet-smelling body finally begin to relax in her arms.

"Will you go with me to the doctor?" Betina asked in a sleepy voice a while later.

Maxine felt such a huge sense of relief rush through her body. She thought she might begin to cry again.

"Yes, baby," she whispered with a hug. They both fell asleep wrapped in each other's arms.

Maxine had been on call Easter Sunday and spent a large part of the day on the phone with several different patients, which put a damper on the festivities at Elaine and Cheryl's house. After the fourth time she was paged, the others at the small party nearly forgot she was even there. On Monday morning, Maxine was surprised when Betina asked for her help that afternoon. Since Betina was no longer insisting that Maxine stay out of it, she called an internal medicine friend while they had some momentum going. Dr. Rose Romero was glad to see them after regular office hours.

Feeling relieved about finally getting this taken care of, Maxine's day went smoothly with a full complement of patients that miraculously stayed on schedule. However, her frustration eventually returned when she finally got home to pick up Betina only to have her pager go off.

"What timing," Maxine said as she kissed Betina on the check before dialing her answering service. "This is probably the Alvarez baby again." Maxine watched Betina go through hangers in the closet looking for something to wear. "Dr. Weston returning a page," she said into the phone when the service answered. She listened and wrote down the phone number they gave her. Sylvia Alvarez had already gone into false labor two days earlier. Maxine called her patient and got an older woman on the phone.

"*Hola.*"

"Dr. Weston here. Can I speak with Sylvia Alvarez, please?"

"Doctor! You called so quickly! It's my daughter! The baby is coming!"

"How far apart are the contractions?"

Maxine was so focused on her patient, she didn't even notice when Betina finally got dressed.

"I'll meet you at the Emergency Room at the Methodist Hospital," Maxine said. "Sounds like he's really on his way this time." She hung up the phone and then out of habit, checked her pager again. She found Betina in the bathroom putting the finishing touches on her makeup. *I'll have to reschedule her appointment now*, Maxine thought. *I promised to go with her.*

"I'm sorry, but I have to go, baby," Maxine said as she kissed the back of Betina's neck.

"I know." Betina turned around. "Isn't Dr. Romero's office in the complex next to the Methodist Hospital?"

Maxine suddenly felt such a huge sense of relief rush through her at Betina's interest in keeping the appointment anyway. *Major break-through here*, she thought. *Major, major, major.*

"Yes," she said, taking Betina into her arms. "I might have time to get you there and introduce you to her, but I won't be able to stay. I can call her and see if we can reschedule for tomorrow if that's better, though."

"No," Betina said. She stepped back away from her and reached for a tube of lipstick on the vanity. "I'm ready now. I can go by myself."

"Betina—"

"Really," Betina said. Their eyes met in the bathroom mirror. "If I'm going to do this, Maxie, I need to do it now." She offered a weak smile. "I might not have the courage again if I wait. I want to make you proud of me."

"I'm already proud of you." She gave Betina an impulsive hug. "I'll always be proud of you."

Betina followed Maxine to the hospital in her own car since Maxine could possibly be stuck at the hospital for hours. Betina had a problem finding a parking place even though it was late in the afternoon, but Maxine parked easily in a slot marked for doctors. Traffic had been horrendous, but they managed to make good time anyway. Maxine called the team center at the emergency department to see if Sylvia Alvarez had arrived, but she hadn't checked in yet.

"Can someone page me when she does?" Maxine asked the clerk.

"If I see her I can."

"That's okay. I'll be over there in about ten minutes."

Betina caught up with her by the elevator in the parking garage. She was stunning in a long embroidered denim dress that buttoned down the front and revealed just a hint of cleavage. Her royal blue sleek leather pumps made her about three inches taller than Maxine. To anyone else, Betina would appear relatively relaxed, but Maxine could tell she was nervous by the way she kept switching her purse from one shoulder to the other while they waited for the elevator.

"How do you know this Dr. Romero?" Betina asked quietly.

"I delivered both of her sons."

They got on the elevator and Betina smiled and leaned against her.

"So you've seen her naked."

Maxine shook her head and chuckled. "Not completely."

Her pager went off again. She checked the number and took her cell phone out of her pocket. They stepped off the elevator as she called her answering service again.

"I can take it from here," Betina said.

"I know you can." Maxine put the small phone up to her ear. "Dr. Weston returning a page."

"Go take care of your patient," Betina said. "I'll see you at home later."

Chapter Twenty

Maxine's patient had been stuck in traffic with a frantic husband driving and a mother who was teetering on the edge of hysteria, and no one wanted to deliver a baby under those conditions. They finally arrived with a police escort—flashers pulsating, sirens wailing, and red lights so urgent and intimidating that they gave Maxine an adrenaline rush she hadn't felt in ages.

A nurse helped a young Mr. Alvarez get his wife into a wheel-chair. The nurse pushed the patient inside and down a short hallway to an OB room located in the emergency department. Maxine wanted to examine her before she sent her up to the obstetrics ward. The thought of having to deliver a baby in an elevator wasn't the least bit appealing to her. She pointed down a hallway, indicating to the pale husband and the patient's mother where the waiting area was.

"Someone will be with you shortly," she told them.

Maxine went into the OB room and began washing her hands in the sink just inside the door. "How are you doing, Sylvia?"

"He's coming for sure this time, Dr. Weston. I'm so glad we made it here!"

The nurse had already helped Sylvia into a hospital gown and had hoisted her up on the examining table. Maxine closed the door with her foot and sat down on the rolling stool the nurse positioned at the end of the table. Sylvia began to yell at the onset of another contraction.

"Oh, my," Maxine said as she took her first look. "Let's get her upstairs now."

An hour later, Maxine had already delivered a healthy baby boy and enjoyed seeing the look of relief and excitement on the young father's face when she found him in the waiting area on the obstetrics ward.

"How's my wife?"

"She's tired, but fine."

"When can I see her?"

He had elected not to be present in the delivery room. He was still shaken from the drive to the hospital, but the patient's mother had been in the delivery room.

"You can ask them right over there at the desk," Maxine said as she pointed toward the nurse's station. "Congratulations, Mr. Alvarez." She looked up and was surprised to see Betina and Dr. Rose Romero at the end of the hallway, talking to one of the nurses. Maxine waved and met them halfway. "What are you two doing here?"

"We're looking for you," Rose said. "We thought it might be possible to catch a few words with you."

"In between contractions and all that heavy breathing that goes on up here?" Maxine said with a laugh. She gave Rose a hug. A petite woman in her mid-thirties, Maxine saw her once a year as a patient, but met her in passing in the hospital cafeteria or the parking garage a few times a week. Maxine also received several referrals from her when Rose's patients needed an ob-gyn consultation.

"How far along is your patient?" Rose asked.

"Actually, she almost delivered on the way to the hospital, but made it here on time. She and her new son are doing well."

"Then is there some place around here where we can talk?" Rose asked. "Or we can go back to my office if that's easier."

Maxine found an empty break room around the corner. There was a table with four chairs, an ice machine, a coffee maker, a refrigerator, and a television mounted on the wall. The TV was on, but the sound was off.

"How's this?" Maxine asked. She was curious as to why they had gone to so much trouble to find her. "I'm sorry I couldn't be there to at least introduce you two."

Rose sat down at the table. "Betina found my office without any problem. She has the paperwork to get some tests done in the morning. I should have the results back by the end of the week."

"Good," Maxine said. She glanced over at Betina, who was sitting beside her with her hands folded on top of the table. Betina looked straight ahead, focusing on an empty coffee pot on the counter. Maxine reached over and touched her hands. "Are you okay?"

Startled, Betina nodded, indicating that she was fine.

"I guess I don't understand why we're here," Maxine said. *Betina could have told me all of this at home later,* she thought.

"Betina wanted to make sure you knew she had seen me," Rose explained.

"What?"

"There was some sort of misunderstanding about a previous appointment?"

"So you're both over here for that?" Maxine asked.

"Betina thought it was necessary that the three of us meet."

"I see," Maxine said. She felt a bit uncomfortable at the implication that maybe she didn't trust Betina to take care of this on her

150

own. Maxine thought of it as a subject better left handled between the two of them without involving a stranger. To have Rose know something so personal about them already was somewhat unnerving. *But this isn't about you,* she reminded herself. *This is about Betina and what's best for her.*

Maxine took a few seconds to look closely at her lover and didn't like the way Betina was acting at the moment. She had a blank expression and glazed-over look in her eyes that Maxine had never seen before. She reached for Betina's hand again. "Are you sure you're okay?"

Betina continued to stare at the coffee pot on the counter.

"Betina," Maxine said a little louder. "Can you hear me?"

Betina turned to Rose and said, "Tell her what we discussed earlier."

Maxine let go of the breath she'd been holding. *What in the world is wrong with her?*

"Betina wanted to make sure you were informed about the things she and I discussed," Rose said. "As you suspected, there are indications that she's depressed. I asked her a few questions about new sleep habits, and decreases in her energy level, concentration, or changes in appetite. I'm ordering some tests, to include a complete blood count, as well as blood sugar, serum electrolytes, and thyroid function tests. After I get the results back, we'll see where we want to go from there."

Maxine could feel her heart beating inside her chest. Something wasn't right and she couldn't shake the fear that began traveling through her body. Then she remembered how Joey had described Betina's bouts of silent defiance when they were younger. Now Maxine wondered if Betina's silence had been traumatically induced, or if it had been a willful way for her to make a statement to those she felt had wronged her.

"Betina also mentioned her dislike for therapy," Rose continued. "There are a number of good psychiatrists and therapists in town. I think we can find one that she can feel comfortable with."

151

Maxine kept watching her lover with concern. *She's ignoring me!* Maxine thought suddenly. *What the hell is going on here?*

"I have the utmost confidence in the psychiatrists and therapists on my referral list," Rose added.

Feeling the same way about the physicians she regularly sent her own patients to, Maxine had to agree. "If we have to weed through a dozen therapists, we'll just check them off one at a time," she said with a reassuring smile.

Betina turned to Rose and said, "There's no other way? I have to have a shrink?"

"It's—"

"Why can't one of you just prescribe whatever it is you think I need?"

"Depression is very common," Rose said. "Max and I deal with it every day in our patients. But psychiatrists are trained specifically to treat depression and a number of other similar or related conditions. There could be underlying problems that need to be addressed that are causing the depression, or there could be a number of other reasons for it. The drugs being used now need to be monitored and properly adjusted. A psychiatrist is better trained to do that."

"What if my only problem turns out to be therapy and having to go to a shrink?" Betina asked. She kept her eyes on Rose and didn't even seem aware that Maxine was there in the room with them. "What if the main thing making me depressed is the thought of going back into therapy?"

Rose arched her eyebrows and shrugged. "Then I'd say we have a problem."

Betina rolled her eyes and mumbled, "Well . . . *duh!*"

Maxine wasn't sure what to do once she got home. Betina had sped past her when they left the hospital parking garage, and had arrived home first. When Maxine got there, she found Betina in the dark, sitting on the sofa in the living room. Maxine switched on the lamp by the recliner and noticed that she was drinking a beverage too light in color to be a cola.

"What's the matter, baby?" Maxine asked with concern.

Betina stared straight ahead then slowly took a long drink from the glass.

"Betina."

Maxine got no response from her. She went behind the sofa and reached over the back of it and took the glass out of her hand. She could smell the bourbon before she even got it up to her nose. They didn't keep hard liquor in the house. Neither of them were drinkers, but when and if they did drink, they only had wine.

"Where did you get this?" Maxine asked.

She went to the kitchen to empty the glass. To Maxine's surprise, Betina followed her, opened the cabinet and got down another glass. She then went to the pantry and took out a small bottle of Southern Comfort, opened it up, and filled the new glass.

Maxine went to the pantry where she found four other bottles of bourbon on the shelf next to some soup and pasta. *What the hell . . . ,* she thought. Maxine turned around to say something, but Betina wasn't there. She followed her back to the living room and saw her sitting on the sofa again, drinking and staring at the stereo.

"What happened, baby?" Maxine whispered, confused. It wasn't until she spoke that she realized she was crying. "You were fine two hours ago." She came closer and took the second glass away from her. Betina didn't resist, move or say anything.

"You were even fine a few weeks ago," Maxine said. "Tell me what's going on." She sat down next to her on the sofa and put her arm around her. Maxine felt the lump in her throat grow larger when Betina put her head on Maxine's shoulder. They stayed that way for a long time. Maxine reached over and took her hand and laced their fingers together.

Finally, Betina said, "Have you ever seen real pornography?"

With eyes wide and a flashback of her recent conversation with Joey, Maxine thought about the question for a moment before answering no. "Nothing more than *Penthouse* or *Playboy*." She waited for Betina to say more, but all she did was squeeze Maxine's hand tighter. "A bunch of my friends went to a sleazy theater once in college. Someone wanted to see a porn movie," Maxine said. Their heads were touching now and Betina gripped her hand even that much tighter. "I remember one of them describing how her shoes practically stuck to the floor and that was enough for her. She was out of there." She kissed the top of Betina's head as a tear rolled down her cheek. "Got her money back and left."

"You didn't go with them?"

"I had a test the next day. No time for porn. It wasn't something I was interested in anyway. Lesbian porn maybe, but that's not what they were out looking for."

Maxine waited for Betina to say something else, but at the moment just being held seemed to be the only thing that mattered. A while later Maxine said, "Joey told me about what happened with your parents and the magazines when you two were kids."

Betina sniffed. "He did?" she asked in a small voice. "When did he do that?"

"The other night at the dance. We had a good talk."

"What did he say?"

"He told me what happened. He still gets upset when he talks about it," Maxine said. "That was the first time I'd ever seen him cry."

"Really? He cried?"

"He knows what he did to you that day."

"I'm not sure he does," Betina said quietly. "Have you ever been accused of being a whore?" Her voice broke, but she cleared her throat and gripped Maxine's hand again. "I barely knew what a whore was. I had to look it up later that night to make sure."

"Who called you a whore?"

"My mother. I'd never seen her so crazy before."

"So have you been thinking about all of that recently?"

Betina nodded and sniffed.

"Tell me what you've been thinking, baby. If all of that's being dredged up again, it's no wonder you're depressed."

Betina turned and put both arms around Maxine's neck. "I keep living that day over and over again in my head. Not all the time, but often enough that it's affecting me in some terrible ways. I don't know how to shut those memories off when they come back. I can't get rid of her twisted face and the way she . . ."

Maxine hated hearing Betina cry this way. It tore a hole in her heart to see her in such pain. "It's okay, baby," she whispered into her hair.

"The other day," Betina said. "No, it was a few weeks ago actually. I lose all track of time now."

Maxine kissed the top of her head. Betina's words were a bit slurred from the bourbon she had gulped earlier. "What happened a few weeks ago?"

"I was going through some of the mail at work," Betina said. "A stack of catalogs. We get hundreds of supply catalogs a week and we go through them when we get a chance." Betina pulled a lacy white handkerchief from her pocket and blew her nose and dabbed at her eyes with it. "One of the catalogs was in a brown wrapper and I opened it up. I froze when I saw what it was. I think my heart may have stopped for a while there." An involuntary shiver went through her body. "It was a porn magazine with these thirty-inch penises in it."

"Thirty inches?"

"They *looked* thirty inches."

"Was it Joey's magazine?" Maxine asked. *I'll kick his ass*, she thought.

"No."

With another light kiss on the top of Betina's head, Maxine playfully asked, "Was it yours?"

Betina's unexpected laughter was a relief as she thumped Maxine on the arm. "*No*, it wasn't mine!"

"Okay. Just kidding."

"It was delivered to the wrong address. It belonged to some pervert down the street from the shop." She was quiet again and Maxine waited until Betina was ready to continue. Finally, she said, "I guess I freaked out a little."

"I don't blame you," Maxine said. "Seeing a thirty-inch-long penis would freak me out, too. Tell me what all happened to you that day."

"I don't remember much else about that day. All I know is, I stopped checking the mail after that. At work and here at home. I hated getting mail out of the boxes . . . and . . . and I hated even touching it." Another shiver went through Betina's body as she snuggled closer to her. "Hold me," she whispered.

Maxine pulled her closer.

"That went on for what seemed like weeks and weeks. Then once the thing happened with the electricity getting turned off," Betina said, "I knew I had to get over it. I promised you I would keep up with the mail and I did, but each day since then, I've cried every time I've gone to the mailbox. Now I make Joey go through all the catalogs by himself, just in case there's something I don't care to see in those piles. I won't even touch them." She sniffed again and dabbed her eyes with the handkerchief once more. "So I've still got a ways to go in several areas. Is there such a thing as a catalog phobia? If there is, then that's what I've got."

"Why didn't you tell me any of this before?"

Betina shrugged. "I'm just now beginning to figure things out, Maxie. I thought I was over all of that. I thought I had forgiven Joey and my parents for being so . . . so . . . so mean to me. Then I find an icky magazine in the mail and it's like I'm fourteen years old and being called a whore all over again."

"I'm sorry," Maxine said as she kissed her on the head.

"So can I have my glass back now?"

"The booze? No, I don't think so."

"It's the only thing that makes me feel better."

"We'll find something else that'll make you feel better soon."

"I can't go to another shrink, Maxie," she whispered. "He thought I was a whore, too."

"He said that to you?"

"He didn't have to. I could see it in his eyes."

"I'm sorry you had to go through all of that alone."

"Yeah, me too."

Chapter Twenty-one

Maxine wasn't surprised when Betina called her later in the week to let her know that all the tests were back and she was in fine physical condition.

"That's good to hear," Maxine said. She opened up the bottom drawer of her desk in her office and pulled out a pair of Nike Airs. After being in surgery all morning, her feet appreciated the change. "What does Dr. Romero suggest now?"

"She has a list of shrinks I'm supposed to be considering."

Maxine could hear the dread in Betina's voice.

"I really don't want to do this, Maxie."

"I know, baby." *She's crying*, Maxine realized. *Damn. I hate this.*

"I don't think you do know."

Maxine tucked the phone into her shoulder as she bent down to tie her shoe. "I have an idea how we'll choose a psychiatrist for you, so let's not worry about that right now, okay?"

"I have to pick one of these losers on this list she gave me."

Maxine smiled and finished lacing up both sneakers. Her feet felt almost new again. "We don't know for sure that they're losers yet, babe."

"Whenever I think about a shrink, the word 'loser' pops into my head. My insurance only has a few shrinks they'll let me choose from."

"Don't give that another thought," Maxine said. "We'll find one you like. I promise."

There was a knock on her office door. Mona stuck her head in and nodded toward the right down the hallway. "Got one in the chute."

"Thanks," Maxine said. She stood up and checked her pager out of habit. "Okay, my love. I have patients to see. This evening we'll talk about my plan for finding you a psychiatrist. How about I take you to dinner and we discuss things there?"

She heard a sniff on the other end of the phone. "What about that outrageously expensive 'something' you promised to get for me a few days ago?"

Maxine smiled. "So you'd like to go shopping before dinner?"

"That might help a lot. I'm depressed, you know."

"Yes, I know."

"Well, don't leave home without your credit card, Dr. Weston."

They had four lists of psychiatrists to choose from—the list Maxine routinely used, the list Betina's health insurance used, the list Elaine Marcaluso's office had faxed over, and the one Dr. Romero had given Betina. It wasn't surprising that each list had several of the same names on it. Maxine understood this to be one of the most critical issues facing them now. If Betina couldn't find a psychiatrist she was happy with, then treating her depression would become almost impossible.

They decided to stay in for dinner, with Betina going to a lot of trouble to prepare a meal. Maxine puttered in the kitchen with her, and each time she tried to bring up the subject of finding a psychiatrist, Betina did something to distract her with either a "hand me the garlic powder" or a "taste this and see if it needs more salt." Maxine let her get away with it before and during dinner, but afterward she finally said, "Okay. We've put this off long enough."

"I don't want to talk about it," Betina said, almost whining.

"Well, you have to. This isn't going away by itself. Are you ready for my suggestions?"

Betina got up from the table and took their plates into the kitchen. After setting them in the sink, Maxine followed her, took her hand, and led her to the living room sofa.

"Tell me about your first psychiatrist," Maxine said after they both sat down. "What did he look like then? How old was he?"

"I was a kid," Betina said. "To me he was older than dirt." She paused before adding, "Probably forty-five. Fifty maybe."

"Did he have hair? Was he tall? Short?"

"I mostly saw him sitting down."

"Okay," Maxine said. *This is going nowhere fast*, she thought. Maxine reached for a tablet on the coffee table and pulled a pen from her pocket. "My suggestion is this. We write down all the things you can remember about the old psychiatrist, to include, physical features, accent, attitude, age—everything you can remember. Then we get as much information as we can about each doctor on the referral list. We're aiming for a psychiatrist who is as much *unlike* the one you had before as we can get. Are you with me so far?"

Betina put her head on Maxine's shoulder. "I'm with you."

"Okay, good. Now tell me about him, baby," Maxine said in a quiet voice. "Tell me everything you can remember."

As Betina began to talk, Maxine took notes. The anger Maxine heard in her voice made it even more apparent just how deeply hurt and troubled Betina still was over the magazine and forced-therapy incidents. She wanted to help her lover through this any way she could. For Maxine, nothing else mattered.

160

"He always had a stack of folders on his desk," Betina said. "All he did was work on things while I was there."

"No interaction with you at all?"

"Not that I remember. Oh! The first day I went to his office he asked me to draw a picture of my family. That's the one and only conversation I remember us having." She straightened the bottom of her dress in a nervous gesture that made Maxine smile. "He might've thought I was a smart-ass in addition to a whore, though. It was hard to tell. Not to mention the fact that I was always so furious for having to be there to begin with."

"Tell me about the picture you drew for him."

"Two big stick figures holding hands with a boy stick figure," Betina said. "I gave the boy a cowlick just like the one Joey used to have. I had the three of them on the beach looking out at the water. I showed the backs of their heads and had the boy stick figure standing on some magazines." Betina shrugged. Her voice sounded more normal than it had all evening—almost mischievous in its tone and phrasing. "But I'm not much of an artist, so I was the only one who knew the boy stick figure was standing on porn magazines."

They shared light laughter together.

"I thought it was a dumb little assignment and that loser never really asked me anything about it," Betina said. "Just another way for him to pass the hour and collect his money."

"That's how you felt then?"

"Yes. I'm sure that's how I'll feel now when I have to go back into therapy. There's no telling what kinds of things the loser told my parents. All I remember is they thought he was great."

"Hmm," Maxine said. She held up the tablet and glanced over her notes. "I have another idea that might help." She put the pen back in her pocket. "Suppose we just find a psychiatrist who will monitor your medication if you need it and ask a few questions once a month. Then we'll look for a good psychologist to help you sort through your other problems." Maxine reached over and gave her hand another squeeze. "Maybe we'll look for a lesbian psychologist.

161

Someone who can really understand you as a person and identify with your sexuality. This community is full of lesbian therapists."

"And we already know most of them socially."

Maxine shrugged. "That's true."

"Like I said before, I'm not sure I want to share any of this with someone I know," Betina said.

"We're just brainstorming here, baby. We're not making any decisions yet. You need to give it a chance, okay?"

"Yeah, yeah, yeah."

"We can't keep beating the same dead horse. At some point we need to move forward. Tell me what you're thinking right now."

Betina shrugged. "I don't feel comfortable with how it's so acceptable to have to pay someone to listen to you. People should want to listen to others for free."

"You mean like friends or relatives?" Maxine asked.

"I don't know. The thought of having to pay someone to listen to my problems just doesn't sit well with me. The whole idea of therapy just makes me uneasy."

"They won't just be listening to you," Maxine said. "They'll try and help you figure things out."

"That other loser didn't try and do anything for me."

"You didn't have the right analyst, baby. A lot of thought and research should go into finding the right therapist. Some could be good for *you*—and then be bad for someone else. It's like buying a new car. You should choose one and drive it first, then see if it meets all your needs." Maxine leaned over and shuffled through a few things on the coffee table and came up with a copy of *WomanSpace*, the local lesbian paper. "Maybe we can find a lesbian therapist in here that neither of us knows. If nothing else, we might be able to get a referral from one of them that could be helpful."

"So I really have to do this?"

"Yes, baby. You really have to do this," Maxine said.

❦

The next day Maxine placed calls to a number of lesbian thera-pists in San Antonio. It didn't surprise her that they all had a large client base. She left messages on a number of answering machines and made herself available for their return calls.

Lesbians and therapy seem to just go together, she thought. After answering several phone calls, she got the name of a therapist that was new to the area. Since Maxine and Betina were so well known in the community, it was a relief to finally write down a name she had never heard of before. Maxine gave Laverne Simon a call and set up an early evening appointment for them.

"You'll probably get paged as soon as we get there," Betina said as she locked the front door of their house that evening.

"I'm not on call," Maxine said. "I have the night off."

"Then I can surely think of other things I'd rather be doing with you."

Maxine smiled. "Then we'll just have to do them later."

"Let's take my car," Betina said. "If we show up in a Jag, she might jack up her prices on me." She handed Maxine the keys to her car. "Here. You drive. I can feel myself getting all mad and cranky already."

Maxine opened the car door for her. "No need to get cranky. It'll be okay. She sounded harmless on the phone."

They found the address in a nice, secluded neighborhood in one of the older, more well-established suburbs. The street was quiet and gave the impression of a retirement community—no toys on the manicured lawns. Maxine parked in front of the house and opened her car door. She glanced over at Betina, who was stiff as a post and staring straight ahead. Maxine reached over and touched her.

"Come on, baby. We're here."

"I can't do it," Betina mumbled.

"I'll be with you the whole time. If you don't like her, then we never have to see her again, okay?" Maxine got out of the car and went around to the passenger's side to open the door for her, but before she got there, Betina reached back and locked the door.

163

"Well, crap," Maxine muttered. With the car alarm on the key ring, she locked all the doors and set the alarm. Then she deactivated the alarm and opened all the doors again.

"It was worth a try," Betina said when Maxine finally got her out of the car.

"Sometimes you're just cute as hell, you know that?" Maxine said with a chuckle.

Chapter Twenty-two

Laverne Simon, wearing a cotton floral print dress, was an older woman with a loose bun of steel-gray hair on top of her head. Like a little storage rack for convenience, she had a pencil tucked behind her ear and glasses perched on her head. At five-feet-seven, she was almost as tall as they were. She had expressive blue eyes and made them feel welcome right away with a smile and warm greeting.

"I'm Betina Abbott. The one with all the problems," Betina said, "and this is my partner, Dr. Maxine Weston."

"It's nice to meet you both. Come in, please. Let me just put Scooter out or he'll be begging for attention," Laverne said, indicating the small gray poodle wagging its nub of a tail. She walked across a huge open room that had a nice arrangement of couches, love seats, and a recliner in the sitting area.

"Don't disturb the dust," Laverne said. "It protects the furniture."

A sliding glass door led outside to a small backyard, enclosed by an exceptionally tall wooden privacy fence. Plants of all types and sizes covered the landscape and surrounded a gurgling fountain. Flagstone and other types of flat rocks carved several paths, replacing grass and native vegetation. Maxine noticed some patio furniture and an assortment of birds that fluttered for cover as soon as the glass door slid open to let the poodle out. From where Maxine stood, she could also see a pair of golden pheasants, a peacock and a few other colorful ground birds. The poodle went outside without giving the birds a thought.

"Oh, Maxie," Betina said with a small gasp. "Look at how beautiful they are!" She reached for Maxine's hand as the three women stood there watching the birds.

"The peacocks are new," Laverne said. "I just got them last week, but they seem to be adjusting well to city life."

"They're beautiful," Betina said.

"Thank you. Let's go back to my office."

"Does Maxie have to come with us?" Betina asked. "Can she stay here and wait?"

"Of course," Laverne said. "Make yourself comfortable, Dr. Weston."

Maxine was surprised by Betina's request. *She doesn't want me to go in with her?* Maxine thought. *Hmm. That was quick.*

Betina must've seen the perplexed expression on her face. "I'll be okay," she said. "I feel good here."

Maxine nodded and felt the tension practically draining from her body. As she watched them walk across the room and then disappear into another part of the house, Maxine realized Betina had cleared another major hurdle. She turned back toward the sliding glass door and watched the antics of the menagerie in Laverne Simon's backyard.

After a while, Maxine made herself comfortable on the love seat and then placed a few calls on her cell phone. She made a date with Elaine Marcaluso to meet for breakfast at their usual place in the morning and then called her parents in Connecticut. She got their answering machine as usual. A while later she heard scratching and whining at the patio door, but wasn't sure about letting the dog in. *He's probably just lonely*, she thought.

Maxine went outside with him and sat down in one of the lawn chairs on the patio. The cool April air felt good and she enjoyed watching the birds with Scooter seemingly content lying at her feet. The yard sloped upward toward the back fence, and the serenity fountain was a nice mixture of water-over-rock and a bubbling pool in the center of the yard. She had forgotten how calming the sound of water could be and decided to have a few small gurgling fountains put in both her offices at home and at work.

A while later, Betina and Laverne found her outside. Betina's laughter warmed Maxine's heart.

"I thought you'd left me here," Betina said.

Maxine laughed. "I couldn't resist this wonderful place. Scooter and I have been bonding."

"I spend as much time as I can out here," Laverne said.

"Why don't the birds fly away?" Betina asked.

"Occasionally they do, but they usually come back or a neighbor brings them back." She bent down to give the dog a pat on the head. "Scooter's job is to keep cats out of the yard."

Maxine smiled at the dog and then stood up. "Everything go okay?" she asked her lover.

Betina reached for her hand. "Yes, it did. Better than I ever expected. I have two appointments with her this week. It looks like I have a lot to talk about. Laverne also mentioned that we might benefit from having a few sessions with her as a couple at some point in the future."

Maxine nodded and wasn't opposed to the idea. "Whatever you think is best," she said to Laverne.

"I also told her that it's okay for you to know everything that's going on with me during my sessions," Betina said. She gave Maxine's hand a light squeeze. "I felt better having you know what was happening when I saw Dr. Romero. Talking things over with you helps me process all this information. It's all so overwhelming sometimes."

Maxine's heart filled with warmth and emotion. She gave her lover an impulsive hug while Scooter wagged his tail at their feet.

Maxine couldn't believe how much better she felt as they drove away from Laverne Simon's house. Just knowing Betina had found a therapist she liked seemed to lift both their spirits.

"She's got a fountain in her office that just had me so relaxed," Betina said before they were even a block away. "It's a good thing I didn't have to pee! But I loved it. There was just so much positive energy in that room."

Maxine explained how she had made some phone calls then decided to join Scooter on the patio. "The time seemed to fly by while I was out there."

"That backyard was just so cool," Betina said. "Well, aren't you gonna ask me what we talked about for an hour?"

"I'm anxious and eager to hear how it went."

"I've got no secrets from you now, darlin'. I told that to Laverne, too. If something comes up, I told her I didn't mind the two of you discussing me and my problems. Once I busted myself on the witch doctor herbs and Joey's flappin' lips told you about the porn magazines, you know about all there is to know about me."

"I doubt that. So what did you two talk about?" Maxine asked.

"You."

"Me?"

Betina turned to look at her. "You and how wonderful you are to me. How lucky I am to have you in my life." She looked down and fiddled with a button on her blouse. "How hard you've been trying to get me some help. How much trouble you went to on Valentine's Day. You, you, you, darlin'."

Maxine gulped. "You told her about the haunted house ride?"

168

"And the Ferris wheel."

"Oh, my." Maxine said with a laugh. When they first met people, they usually worked up to such revelations.

"I needed to see her reaction to some of the things I told her, so I gave her some stories to ponder."

"And? Did she pass your test?"

Betina laughed. "Yeah. She did and she had a few stories of her own. She told me about a girlfriend she had once who decided to get frisky with her on the back of a bus. The driver slammed on the brakes to miss a pedestrian and threw them both on the floor." Betina's delighted laughter made Maxine laugh, too. "She said after that, the moment was gone." She reached for Maxine's arm and looped hers through it. "Laverne told me I'll probably need medication for depression plus therapy for gaining better coping skills and a full recovery, if there is such a thing. She wants me to see a shrink for the meds, so she'll help me with that, too. I like Laverne. She made me feel important. She made me think that what I had to say actually mattered, unlike that loser of a shrink my parents spent a fortune on when I was a kid."

Maxine leaned over and kissed her cheek. She didn't bother to tell her that all therapy should make the patient feel important for at least an hour. Betina and her parents were robbed.

Maxine found a parking place close to the door of the coffee shop. Elaine's car was there already.

"Yes on the Spurs tickets," Maxine said. "Let me give you the money for them now while I have some cash on me, and you can keep our tickets for us so I'll know where they are."

"You look a little frazzled there, Dr. Weston."

Maxine smiled. "Late night. Don't ask."

"I wouldn't dream of it," Elaine said with a laugh.

Maxine thought, *"She" was out again last night. My Betina enjoys herself so much when that happens.*

"Well, whatever happened, it must've been good from the look on your face," Elaine said, peeking over the top of her menu.

"It was sexual in nature, and I'm sure you don't want to hear about it."

"You would be right."

"Do we have good seats or bad seats for the game?"

"Semi-good."

"Will eighty bucks cover us?" Maxine asked as she slid the money across the table.

"Yeah, that should do it."

The waitress came to take their orders. After she left, Elaine asked, "How often do lesbian couples have sex? I mean *regular* lesbian couples. Not you and Betina."

"The stats I've read aren't promising. Why? Are you and Cheryl watching more late night TV than you used to?"

"We're still going strong at a steady two or three times a week."

"Damn, girl! That's great!"

"I find myself enjoying the intimacy of just being held and feeling her close to me during the night." Elaine took a sip of her coffee. "I can see where lesbians can be quite content with more of that and less of the 'bone jumping' thing."

Maxine nodded. "I know what you mean. There's more to life and there's more to being a couple than having sex."

"Well, listen to you being all philosophical about it." Elaine laughed.

"Sex without intimacy is just sex. You can get that from having sex with yourself," Maxine said. "But sex with intimacy is called making love, and there's a big difference in making love and having sex."

"Well said."

"I've only had sex with Betina once or twice. That was when we were first together. It's been different each and every time after that." Maxine stirred her coffee. "Whether we're getting it on in the last row of a movie theater or in a dressing room in a department store.

170

With each encounter now, there's intimacy in our lives because we love each other."

Elaine sighed heavily and shook her head. "Maybe Cheryl and I need to get out more."

Maxine got home at a reasonable hour and could smell sautéed onions in the air. Her stomach growled and she felt warm and loved inside.

"Hi, babe," Betina said. "Day two of therapy. I really like Laverne."

"What did you two accomplish today?"

"She agreed to set out some of our business cards on a table in her office. That was the main thing. Then we discussed my opinion of psychiatrists and my previous experiences with therapy. Psychiatrists . . . psychologists . . . it's just all so confusing some-times."

"The psychiatrist is the one who will prescribe the medication."

"Yeah, yeah, yeah."

"Did you and Laverne have a good session today? Any break-through there?"

"Major breakthrough," Betina said. "Laverne has a friend who's a shrink. Since it looks like I'll need to be on medication for this depression crap, then I at least want a shrink Laverne has confidence in. We talked about the shrink most of the session. I have an appoint-ment with her next week." Betina plopped a hunk of butter into the skillet as she continued stirring the steaming concoction. "The shrink isn't on my list of providers for my insurance, so I'm bummed out about that."

"If you like her," Maxine said, "don't worry about it. I'll take care of it."

"I still want to take a look at the shrinks on my provider list," Betina said. She stopped stirring the onions and set the wooden spoon down on the counter. "I might be depressed for the rest of my life, Maxie. It might never go away."

"I know."

"It doesn't seem fair."

"How are you feeling overall?"

"I'm tired and I have no reason to be." Betina picked up the wooden spoon and adjusted the burner on the stove.

"We had a pretty wild night. I've been tired today, too."

Betina smiled. "We've had a bazillion nights like that and I've always managed to get up and face the day without whining. That's the difference now," Betina said. "I feel whiny all the time and I hate it. Ordinary things that I used to do without even thinking are now a pain-in-the-ass chore."

"I think that's called 'getting older', my love."

"Well," Betina said. "Getting older sucks."

After dinner they sat on the sofa together with the TV on, but neither was really watching it. Maxine had her head in Betina's lap and caught herself nodding off every few minutes or so.

"I think I'll give this one a try," Betina said.

Maxine's eyes flew open, then she tried to fake attentiveness. "One what, babe?"

"This shrink on my provider list. I need to take responsibility for my own health. Not depend on you to bail me out."

"What?"

"I have insurance," Betina said. "They'll cover this . . . this . . . this condition I have. What if my new shrink decides to put me on medication? None of that's covered if I have a doctor that's not approved by my insurance company."

"If you find a doctor you like from that list, then that's great," Maxine said, trying to sound totally awake. "Just don't settle for a doctor because that's all you think you have to choose from."

Betina smoothed Maxine's hair back from her forehead.

"Thank you, darlin'," Betina said, "but I need to get a grip and stop being such a baby. I want you to save your money for something *big*."

"How big?" Maxine asked. She turned over on her back and stretched.

"Oh, I don't know. I'm still thinking on it."

Betina slipped her hand inside Maxine's shirt and worked her fingers up into her sports bra. Maxine arched her back and couldn't imagine her life being any better.

Chapter Twenty-three

"Dang! These seats have either gotten smaller or my butt's getting bigger," Phoebe said.

"The seats are the same size they've always been," Elaine said. "What size pants are you wearing these days?"

The other five women laughed, but Phoebe didn't think it was funny. As Maxine sat down in her seat, she had to agree with Phoebe—the seats seemed to be smaller than she remembered.

"Hey, at these prices, I shouldn't have to carry around goose-grease just to get me in and out of my seat," Phoebe complained.

"Stay put," Elaine said. "I'll go get you anything you want. Save your goose-grease for another time."

"That's not the point."

"And if she won't get things for you," Cheryl said, "then I'm sure one of us will."

"Still not the point," Phoebe grumbled. "Besides, what if I have

174

to pee in a hurry?" she asked, craning her neck to locate the nearest exit.

"Sorry," Cheryl said. "We can't fix that one for you."

"Then I guess you won't be having any beer tonight," Elaine said with a laugh.

Maxine helped Betina get settled by holding her drink, purse, and binoculars while she wiggled into her seat. That morning Betina had paid her second visit to the psychiatrist she had selected. Maxine was hoping she would tell her how things had gone, but so far Betina hadn't been very forthcoming with information from either visit. Betina had also been uncharacteristically quiet during dinner with their friends, but Maxine tended to attribute that to Blanche and Phoebe monopolizing the conversation.

"You okay, baby?" Maxine leaned over and whispered.

"More or less."

"You're a real chatterbox tonight."

"You want the truth?" She took her purse from Maxine and set it under the seat, then began scanning the crowd with the binoculars. "I want a drink."

Maxine looked down and realized she was still holding both of their cups. "Well, here. Have one."

Betina lowered the binoculars and glanced over at her. "A watery Diet Coke isn't what I had in mind, but thanks anyway."

"You know that with this new medication the doctor put you on, you shouldn't consume any alcohol."

"Yeah, that's what she told me." Betina set the binoculars in her lap and pursed her lips. "But these new pills could take weeks to start working, when a nice shot of bourbon would make me feel better in a matter of minutes."

Maxine didn't say anything. She hadn't considered the possibility that Betina would still want to take up drinking again. That made her almost as nervous as those recurring bouts of silence Betina kept slipping into.

"Sorry you asked?" Betina whispered in her ear.

"No," Maxine said. She wished they were home. She wasn't in the mood for basketball, a complaining Phoebe, or being among a crowd of twenty thousand screaming Spurs fans.

"I don't like feeling this way, Maxie."

"I know."

Betina leaned toward her so their heads were touching.

"You want to go home?" Maxine asked.

After a moment Betina sniffed. "What? And miss seeing the Silver Dancers in those short skirts and all that bad hair?"

The month of May arrived with Maxine covering her patients as well as those of her vacationing partner's. She put in long hours and didn't leave the office until she was caught up. Historically, April and May were not a busy month for deliveries, but there were still a lot of patients to see for prenatal care and gynecological surgeries. The patients she saw for Dr. Clarkson were either emergencies or urgent, but there were enough of both to keep Maxine moving along at a steady pace. For her, what made all the exhausting extra work worth it was the fact that she and Betina would be vacationing at some point in the future and Dr. Clarkson would then be doing the same thing for her and her patients. It eventually all evened out.

Maxine's thoughts continued to drift to Betina. She still hadn't heard too much about Betina's new psychiatrist, but Maxine was glad that she liked the woman well enough to keep going back to her. Dr. Nora Miller was a name Maxine was familiar with, but didn't use as one of her own referrals. Betina had been seeing her twice a week and then would meet with Laverne Simon two other days out of the week. Betina had stated more than once that she felt as though she needed this much counseling and both healthcare professionals accommodated her requests. Maxine wondered if Betina was trying to cram in all that therapy in hopes of getting to the real source of her depression, but Maxine refrained from commenting on that and let Betina and her team of analysts help her work through the problems. Betina spoke frequently about her conversations with Laverne Simon, but seldom mentioned her psychiatrist. All Betina had said in references to Dr. Miller was that she seemed interested in hearing about Betina's sex drive, her relationship with Maxine and the relationship she had with her brother.

One evening as Maxine pulled into the garage at home, she leaned her head back against the headrest and was glad to finally be still for a few moments. She closed her eyes for just a second and woke up with a start when Betina rapped on the car window.

"Are you okay, baby?"

Embarrassed, Maxine shut off the ignition and opened the door. "Holy moly. How long have I been out here?"

"I thought I heard you, but then when you didn't come in the kitchen, I got worried!"

"That's what I get for buying such a comfortable car, I guess." Maxine glanced at her watch and was shocked to see that she had been asleep for nearly ten minutes. Once they were in the kitchen, Maxine stretched and said, "I feel great after that little power nap."

They shared a laugh and Betina slipped into her arms and kissed her. "Dinner's almost ready. Hold me for a few minutes."

Maxine tightened her arms around her and loved the way Betina seemed to fit so perfectly against her. A while later she helped set the table and they both began to slowly unwind.

"You must've had another busy day," Betina said.

"I can't remember the last time the waiting room was so full, but I eventually got around to everyone. So how was your day?"

Their schedules were similar now. Betina worked later in the afternoon to make up for her early appointments with her therapists. There were days when Maxine actually got home first when Betina had clients scheduled later in the afternoon.

"Laverne and I are making some headway on a lot of things," Betina said. "We just have the best time together. We laugh so much I think she hates taking my money."

Maxine smiled and thought, *I bet she doesn't.*

"Dr. Miller only wants to see me once a week now. The weekly visits will last about another month and then I'll only have to see her once a month after that. She wants to make sure the Zoloft is doing what it's supposed to do," Betina sighed. "Dr. Miller says I should stay on my medication even after the gloom has lifted."

"Depression recurs repeatedly in four out of five patients even if it's for short episodes," Maxine said. "If you stay on the meds, you're only half as likely to have another bout of depression. How are you feeling on the Zoloft?"

Betina shrugged. "Okay, I guess. Maybe even better than I realize. The hardest part is remembering to take it. I'm not used to taking pills. I keep them by the coffee maker so I'll at least see the pill bottle every morning, since nothing's going to keep me from my coffee."

"I've noticed a difference in your energy level already," Maxine said as she cut into her steak, "and I bet Joey has, too."

"Dr. Miller also says that if someone needs medication to get better, they'll more than likely need it to stay better. I'm not looking forward to being on this stuff forever."

"When someone has recurrent episodes of depression, these same drugs can be used as preventive medicine," Maxine said.

"Yeah, yeah, yeah. There's another thing I thought about that's bothering me, too," Betina said. "I don't think about sex very much anymore. Before Dr. Miller put me on these zombie pills, I wanted it all the time. Now I can go for hours and not think about it."

"Hours?" Maxine said with a laugh. That made her stop and think. *When was the last time we made love?* Cuddling in bed and a deep kiss or two on the way out the door in the morning were the only things she could remember happening between them lately. *Oh!* she thought. *That night after the Spurs game! In the parking lot while we waited for the traffic to clear out some. Whew! What a great time they had together.*

"When was that Spurs game we went to?" Maxine asked after a moment.

"Two weeks ago," Betina said.

Maxine looked up from her plate. "What? No way!"

"Two weeks ago," Betina repeated.

We've never gone that long without making love, Maxine thought. *Hmm. Maybe it's because we're both working long hours and we're a lot more tired than usual.*

"How about we forget about you pretending to watch a movie with me after dinner and we open up the drapes and give the neighbors a show on the sofa?" Betina suggested. Her lusty chuckle made Maxine laugh as well.

"That sounds good to me."

After dinner, Maxine helped her clean up the kitchen and get things ready for the next day. As they piddled side-by-side, Maxine felt content in the way their lives were going. The changes she had noticed in Betina over the last week or so were slight, but encouraging. Betina took the time to fix more elaborate meals for them in the evenings and she seemed to have more patience and energy. They both enjoyed being at home and spending time together. Maxine knew for sure things were looking up when she found a note from their new housekeeper the week before asking if her services were still needed, since the place was in such good shape. For Maxine, it felt like the old Betina was back, and she was relieved to know they had weathered such an emotional storm together.

"I'm not sure we should be using the same pool service this year," Betina said as she turned on the dishwasher and neatly folded a hand towel by the sink. "It's almost warm enough now to use and if you'll remember, I caught him sleeping in a chaise on the patio late last fall."

"That's right!" Maxine said. "I'd forgotten about that."

"I'll ask some of my clients and see who they're using. In another few weeks or so it'll be nice to come home from work and be able to go for a swim if we want to."

Maxine realized that it would be very easy for her to slip back into her old habits of letting Betina run the household and take over all those responsibilities, but she didn't want to get caught up in that again. She wanted to do her share around the house, so Maxine volunteered to take care of finding a new pool service as well as the upkeep on the lawn. All she would really have to do is ask Woody what pool service he used, knowing that he would have already done the research. *I've also got resources available to do all this calling and arranging that needs to be done,* Maxine thought. She felt good about taking on more responsibility as far as their personal lives went, even if it actually meant a little more work for her staff at the office.

"This morning Laverne and I talked about the drinking," Betina said as she sat down on the sofa.

Maxine adjusted the drapes and made sure the dining room light was on so there would be soft light filtering into the living room. She perked up at the mention of Laverne's name.

"She had a partner who drank," Betina explained. "She made me see things a lot differently today."

"How so?"

Betina shrugged. "When I was younger, I think I used alcohol more to piss off my parents than anything else. Especially my father. He liked a drink every now and then and each time he wanted one and he found the bottles were either gone or empty, his anger never failed to cheer me up." She chuckled at the memory. "Kids have so little power sometimes. I found a way to get to him and it made me feel important for a few minutes." She smiled. "Even when he was increasing my grounding time another month, it was worth it. You know," Betina said, "I'd never really considered myself high maintenance before, but I guess I kind of am."

Maxine's eyebrows shot up in mock horror. "You're kidding, right? *You?*"

Betina threw her head back and laughed. "You better be careful. I might get my feelings hurt."

180

"I have to say, my love, that you might just be the *only* person who didn't know where you fall on the Maintenance Meter."

Betina nodded and gave her an engaging smile. "Laverne already burst my maintenance bubble today. Apparently I'm *very* high maintenance."

Maxine sat down beside her on the sofa. "You are, but it's never been anything I couldn't handle."

Betina nodded and reached for her hand. "I know."

"And it's never been anything that I didn't *want* to handle."

"I know that, too." Betina brought Maxine's hand up and kissed it. "Laverne thinks my bouts with drinking were my way of getting attention." She lowered her voice and added, "Then and now."

"What are your thoughts on that?"

"I do like a lot of attention."

"I don't give you enough?"

"You do when you have the time," Betina said. "I also know how hard you try to make sure we do have the time. It wasn't an easy session today, Maxie. I cried a lot and even shouted a few times, but Laverne hung in there with me."

"I'm glad she's able to help you work through this. Is there something I'm not doing that you need for me to do?"

"Not that I know of. The really weird thing about this drinking stuff is, I don't like the taste of hard liquor. It's nasty. Might as well be pouring turpentine down my throat. That night I got all those bottles of Southern Comfort and tried to drink them," she said, "I was feeling like a kid again. I was angry at you for making me go see the doctor just like I was mad at my parents for forcing me into therapy. Laverne helped me see that today and it made me feel so ashamed." Betina started to cry softly as she put her head on Maxine's shoulder. "All you were trying to do was help me. I'm such a baby sometimes."

"Your parents were trying to help you, too."

Betina was quiet for a few moments and then said, "Yeah, I guess they were. If maturity came in a bottle, I'd need a whole case of it just to catch up."

"More like a warehouse."

"Well, gee thanks!" Betina said as she snuggled in closer to her.

"Stop beating yourself up over this," Maxine said. "Alcohol isn't the answer to anyone's problems, even if you're using it to hurt someone. It only complicates things."

"I'd empty the bottles down the sink in my bathroom when I was a kid. Then leave just enough in the bottle so he couldn't have more than a capful. The madder he got," Betina said, "the happier it made me."

They both laughed together for a moment, then Betina raised her head and kissed Maxine lightly on the lips.

"That's pretty messed up," Betina admitted.

"You're one of those people who likes to get even."

"I'd open up a bottle and feel *sooo* powerful as that bourbon or rum or vodka glugged its way down the drain. Yeah, that's pretty messed up." She gave Maxine another kiss. "The neighbors are waiting for us to do something, you know."

"Yeah, I know," Maxine said. "Are you up to it?"

"I'm always up to it."

Maxine reached over and began unbuttoning Betina's blouse. "We're so good that the neighbors smoke a cigarette after we have sex. Old man Gardner across the street is probably shooing his wife off to bed now so he can get the telescope out of the hall closet."

Chapter Twenty-four

Maxine helped Betina get the last of her clothes off and kissed those ample breasts until her nipples quivered.

"Oh, yes, baby. My girls like that. Maybe she'll be out tonight," Betina said with excitement in her voice.

"Maybe," Maxine said. She loved the way Betina got comfortable in the recliner with her legs thrown over the arms of the chair and her body so open and inviting. *Yes*, Maxine thought. *This is the most delightful invitation imaginable.*

"My poor baby," Betina cooed.

Maxine kissed the inside of Betina's thigh and rubbed her cheek against it where her lips had been.

"My poor baby," Betina said again. "You spent all day between other women's legs and here you are at home—"

"No need to feel sorry for me."

Maxine remembered Betina making that reference to a small group of women at one of the First Wednesday Night events they

183

had attended. Someone who had heard Maxine being introduced as "Dr. Weston" asked her what her specialty was. Betina leaned in and announced that her girlfriend spent all day between other women's legs, then added that Dr. Weston was an ob-gyn physician. Betina still enjoyed saying it on occasion, and it no longer embarrassed Maxine to have her daily routine described in such a way.

"Ohh . . . ," Betina said the moment Maxine's tongue touched her center. "Oh, my. That feels good, babe."

Betina's hips started to move automatically and she filled her hands with Maxine's hair.

"Mmm . . . so good," Betina kept saying over and over again before she finally asked, "Is she out?"

Maxine gave the signal indicating no, but kept up the oral stimulation. She was enjoying herself so much she hadn't realized how long they had been at it.

"That feels good, but why can't I come?" Betina asked after a while. "I feel like I'm about to and then it goes away."

Maxine listened, but didn't stop what she was doing. She moved her tongue up high and circled the top of Betina's clitoris.

"There! Ohmigod! There, baby. Don't stop. There, there, there . . ."

Maxine sucked it into her mouth and Betina's hips began to grind against her.

"Oh, yes, baby! Like that. Like that."

Maxine slipped her hands under Betina and grasped her hips, pulling her closer.

"That feels so good," Betina moaned again as she brushed the side of Maxine's face with her fingertips. "Why can't I come? What the hell's going on?"

Again, Maxine didn't stop what she was doing and she knew Betina was enjoying her efforts, but she slowly began to realize that by now Betina usually had at least two orgasms. *Wow*, Maxine thought. *It's the Zoloft she's been taking for her depression.*

Maxine intensified her efforts and continued on for another fifteen minutes or so. She could hear Betina's irritation as she panted and gasped her way through the frustration.

"Why can't I come?" she said. "It feels so damn good, but I'm not . . . I'm not . . . but it feels so *good!*"

A while later, Betina tugged on one of Maxine's ears. "It's okay, baby," she said in a low, dejected voice. "We could go on this way all night."

Maxine reached over and got the shirt she had been wearing earlier and wiped her mouth off with it. "Why are we stopping?"

"We just are."

"One more flick of the tongue might be all she needs."

"I'm out of the mood already."

Wow, Maxine thought. *Now there's a first.*

"It's okay," Betina said. She stood up and raised her arms for Maxine to help her out of the chair.

"This has never happened to me before," Betina said. Her eyes were wide and teary. "I can come anywhere . . . anytime. When I was a kid, I could cross my legs on the school bus and feel the most fabulous things as we rattled along those bumpy San Antonio streets." She headed toward the bedroom like a naked streaker. "On the phone with you when you're away at a conference," she continued. "When I'm at work sometimes before Joey gets there and I'm thinking about what you and I did together the night before, I can take care of myself in a matter of seconds if that's all the time I have." She yanked the covers down on the bed and set her alarm clock. "You know how much I like what you were doing to me."

"Betina—"

"It felt good, Maxie."

"Then that's what you need to remember."

"I don't want to just *feel* good," she barked. "I wanted to *come!*"

"I know." Maxine took a deep breath and wasn't sure what to do next. "Come here and let me hold you," she said and got into bed with her. Their bodies were warm and the cool sheets felt soothing against her skin. Once Betina was in her arms, Maxine imagined everything would be better soon. *All things are possible when we're together like this*, she thought.

"Let's take care of you," Betina said. "Maybe that's what I need."

"In a minute," Maxine said as she kissed the top of Betina's head.

"I've never had that happen to me before, Maxie."

"I know, baby. Have you thought about this? That maybe you made me stop too soon?"

"Hell, you would've been there all *night!*"

Maxine chuckled. "So? You say that like it's a bad thing. Was it feeling good or not?"

"It was. Ohmigod was it ever feeling good, but I wanted the big bang! The payoff! I want to feel my eyes roll back in my head like I always do when you suck on my clit that way. 'Feeling good' is like being given cookie crumbs, Maxie. I don't want the crumbs. I want the whole fuckin' *cookie!*"

"Okay, okay."

"I'm sorry, baby," Betina said with a sigh.

"Don't be sorry." Maxine smoothed her hair away from her lover's forehead. "We can try again in the morning. How about that?"

"And what if it doesn't work then either? My whole day will be shot all to hell."

"You can't think of it that way."

"Dr. Miller and I will be having a *loooong* chat during my appointment this week! You can count on *that!*"

"Maybe it's just going to take you longer to come now. You didn't give it much of a chance tonight, you know."

"You were down there working for forty-five minutes, Maxie! I can have four scream-out-your-name-window-rattling orgasms during that amount of time on a slow night." She sat up straight in bed. "This is just unacceptable! Totally unacceptable."

"Calm down or you'll never get to sleep."

"Sleep? Forget about sleep. Lie down and get ready. At least one of us is having an orgasm tonight."

≈≫

186

The next morning they both got up early enough to take a shower together and attempt to make love again. Betina put her arms around Maxine's neck as the water beat down on them in the shower. Betina opened her legs and Maxine slowly moved her hand lower to touch her.

"It feels so good," Betina whispered in her ear.

"Then stop thinking so much about coming and just enjoy what I'm doing."

After a while when they both got tired of standing in the warm spray, they went into the bedroom without really drying off very well. Betina fell back on the bed and brought Maxine down with her, wrapping her legs around Maxine's back.

"It's not going to happen," Betina announced. "I can tell."

"How can you know that?"

"She's broke."

"What?"

"She's broke, Maxie." Betina stretched her arms out over the pillows and let her legs fall to the side. "Dr. Miller cured my depression, but broke my damn clit in order to do it."

"It's not broken," Maxine said with a light laugh as she rolled off of her. "You said things still felt good."

"If I can't come, then what's the point of feeling good? She's broke."

"Will you listen to what you're saying? Feeling good isn't a bad thing, my love. How about we really give her a good workout tonight? After dinner, we'll take a nice long, hot bath together and have some soft music playing and light some candles."

Betina turned on her side and worked her way into Maxine's arms.

"I'll rub lotion on you and you'll get all pampered and squirmy."

She kissed Maxine lightly on the lips. "Okay," Betina said in a small voice. "But I want an orgasm. Not that 'feeling good' crap."

Maxine laughed and kissed her on the forehead. "Okay. We'll work on getting you an orgasm."

Maxine had patients scheduled all day and received a frantic phone message from Betina at nine-thirty that morning. She was with a patient and had to call her back. Maxine finally reached her thirty minutes later on Betina's cell phone.

"It's official," Betina said. "She's broke. I've tried five times already and I can't make myself come."

Maxine sat down at her desk and rubbed the bridge of her nose in hopes of clearing the fog that suddenly enveloped her. After unsuccessfully trying to decipher the three sentences Betina had just uttered, Maxine finally managed to say, "What?"

"She's broke! I've been trying all morning. *Nothing!* Zip! Zilch! It feels good, but I can't make myself come. And you know what, Maxie? That's the *one* thing I've always been able to depend on. In the first grade they made fun of me for always having my hand up my dress, but the laugh was really on *them!* I knew what I was doing and I was years ahead of my time." Betina started to cry. "This is a disaster, Maxie. A fuckin' tragedy . . . no pun intended."

She seemed to run out of steam after that, but still Maxine waited for the next wave of hysteria. She could hear her breathing on the other end of the phone and took this as an opportunity to say some encouraging words. There was a knock on her office door and then Mona stuck her head in.

"Got one in the chute and one in ultrasound."

Maxine waved. She had to make this quick.

"Betina. Listen to me, honey. You have to stop stressing over this now. You're only making things worse."

"How can things get worse? My *clit's* broke!"

"Stop saying that." Maxine almost caught herself laughing out loud.

"If I can't make her work, then nobody can."

"Don't underestimate the power of your gynecologist girlfriend, my love. I have tricks you haven't even seen yet."

After a moment she heard a sniff and then a tiny voice say, "Really?"

"Really," Maxine said with a smile. "Now keep your hands out of your pants for the rest of the day and let her rest up for Maxie's special treatment later."

In that same tiny voice Betina finally said, "Okay."

"Then it's a date. I have to go now, baby. I'll see you later." She turned off her cell phone and slipped it into her lab coat pocket. *Holy moly*, she thought all the way down the hallway. *A broken clit. Where does she come up with this stuff?*

Chapter Twenty-five

Maxine got home and didn't see Betina's car in the driveway. She went inside and got something to drink. Before she could get to the living room, her cell phone rang. Betina was on her way home and she was furious.

"I waited all day for Dr. Miller to call me and you know what she said once I got her on the phone?"

Before Maxine could reply, Betina stormed in again. "She said it's one of the side effects of this Zoloft crap she put me on. She referred to it as a 'sexual dysfunction.' Hey, I read all that stuff on this drug! I thought that 'sexual dysfunction' thing only applied to men! Not me. No more trouser trouts for the old guys! You know what, Maxie? Being depressed wasn't so bad. At least I had hot sex going for me. How can anyone on this Zoloft stuff *not* be depressed if their clits and peckers no longer work?!"

"Where are you?" Maxine asked. *Please don't be out on the Interstate in this kind of mood*, she thought.

"I'm on my way to see Laverne. I need emergency therapy."

Maxine sighed with relief. "That's probably a good idea."

"I'm so pissed I can hardly think."

"I'll be here . . . uh . . . watching TV and waiting for you."

Betina's laughter sounded refreshing after her Zoloft tirade. "You mean sleeping on the sofa."

Maxine woke up a few hours later; Betina still wasn't home. She stretched her arms over her head and before she got up from the sofa, her cell phone rang.

"Did I wake you?"

"No," Maxine said, "but I haven't been up very long."

"I'm on my way home with Chinese food. I'll be there in a few minutes."

"You're sounding better."

"I feel a little better. Laverne is good. She knows me pretty well. Kind of scares me sometimes."

Maxine set the table and put on some soft music. They had a date and Maxine wanted to create a nice atmosphere for Betina to come home to. When she arrived, Maxine took over and got her seated at the table and opened up all the little containers from the takeout bag.

"Laverne says I have to stay on the medication."

Maxine looked at her and imagined the surprise that was registering on her face. *So she's been considering* not *taking it*, she thought with alarm. Instead, Maxine said, "That's a good idea."

"After my little experiment this morning, I was ready to toss those zombie pills in the river."

"You have to give the medication a chance to do its thing, babe. There's a chemical imbalance—"

"This *thing* we're talking about just so happened to put a huge dent in my sex drive, darlin'. That's no minor side effect. That's a major happening in our lives."

"So we'll deal with it."

"Ha! If I threw those zombie pills in the river, I bet fish couldn't have sex either." Betina sighed. "Let's not talk about it anymore. Seems as though my medication for depression has managed to depress me."

"You'll feel better soon."

"I won't if I can't come, Maxie. I'm beginning to think you don't get it."

"Get what? You'll start to feel better once the medication gets established in your system. It's—"

Betina waved her hand in the air. "That's enough. I've read all that bullshit. I don't want to talk about it. Laverne convinced me to keep taking the pills and to keep seeing Dr. Miller. I'll do it and try not to bitch so much, but I'm not happy, Maxie. Let's get that on the record right up front."

Maxine drew them a warm bubble bath after dinner and coaxed Betina into the tub with her. No matter what Maxine did or said, Betina was unable to loosen up and enjoy herself. Maxine's efforts to pamper and please her weren't working, but she wasn't discouraged. When they got out of the tub, Maxine slowly patted her dry with a nice soft towel and sprinkled a little baby powder on her back. Betina said she was tired and just wanted to go to bed.

"What about Maxie's special treatment?" Maxine asked.

"Not tonight," Betina said. She pulled down the covers and got into bed. "Just hold me."

It was then that Maxine began to worry. Before that moment, she thought for sure that once she showered her with extra attention, Betina would embrace it and eventually things would be back to normal again. *She's depressed*, Maxine reminded herself. *A hot bath and a few kind words won't help anything.*

"How about I rub some of that vanilla pudding lotion on your legs?" Maxine offered. "Might make you relax a little."

"I'm fine. Just hold me."

Maxine got into bed and put her arm around her in a spooning position. She felt confused and unsettled and couldn't remember a time when Betina hadn't wanted to make love. *She's had an emotional day*, Maxine reminded herself. *We'll try again when she's ready.*

After surgery the next morning, Maxine changed out of scrubs and into regular work clothes. A waiting room full of women in various stages of pregnancy greeted her when she arrived at the office. Before she could even set her gym bag down, Mona handed her a stack of messages. Two were from Betina.

"Hi, babe. What's up?" Maxine tucked the phone in between her ear and shoulder as she shuffled through the other messages.

"Still nothing," Betina said. "I tried three times this morning and nothing. Zip. Zilch. It feels good, but I can't make myself come."

Maxine stopped what she was doing and let loose with a low groan. "You can't keep stressing over this, Betina."

"That's easy for *you* to say! Your clit still works."

"Ask Dr. Miller about other medications with less dramatic side effects than Zoloft. Something that might be better suited for you than that one."

"She's not taking my calls."

Hmm, Maxine thought. *That's not very professional.*

"Then see if Laverne can call her for you," Maxine suggested.

"Oh! Good idea. Talk to you later."

Maxine closed her cell phone and put it in her lab coat pocket. *For someone who hated therapy, she sure got over that quickly*, Maxine thought.

There was a knock on her office door and Mona stuck her head in. "Got one ready in ultrasound," she said.

Maxine waved, indicating she would be right there. The rest of the day seemed to fly by with a full schedule of patients. Woody would be back in a few days and all the office craziness would hopefully be over with by then. She was more than ready for her life to return to normal again.

Maxine arrived home and entered an empty house. It smelled fresh and clean with a hint of citrus in the air. The check she had left on the table that morning was gone. She went into the living room and stretched out on the sofa to wait for Betina to come home. It was after nine when Maxine woke up again and there was still no sign of Betina. She called Betina's cell phone, but got no answer. She then called Joey to see if maybe they were together.

"I left the shop late and she was still there," he said. Maxine could hear loud music in the background; it sounded like he was at a bar. "She's arranging her schedule around all those doctor's appointments," he said. "It's kind of interesting how her regular customers seem to like the unconventional hours she's keeping now."

"Okay, thanks."

"Oh, by the way," he said. "She was doing much better for a while there and now she's all snippy again. What's going on? She's not talking about anything either."

"New medication," Maxine said. *And a few sexual issues*, she thought.

"Well, she's showing up at work on time and she's keeping her clients happy, so I guess I'll leave it alone."

After Maxine hung up with him, she called the shop.

"Hair Today."

"Betina," Maxine said. "It's late. When are you coming home?"

"Don't wait up for me, babe."

Maxine felt terribly disappointed. She had wanted to try the romantic music, hot bubble bath and vanilla pudding lotion massage thing again before they attempted to make love that evening.

"How much longer will you be?"

"I'm not sure. You know how it is with hair."

Maxine sighed. "Okay. Then I'll see you when you get home." She hung up and went to bed. When her alarm went off the next morning, Betina was asleep beside her. Maxine hadn't heard her come in during the night.

Maxine was so caught up in her own work that she didn't have much time to try and figure out what Betina was up to. Maxine had a patient with Lupus who was experiencing complications, so she spent a good part of the afternoon playing telephone tag with the patient's rheumatologist. Even at work Maxine felt as though she didn't have control over anything.

For the third evening in a row when Betina claimed to be working late at the shop, Maxine was ready to see for herself just how much work Betina was actually doing. After having fallen asleep on the sofa waiting for her to come home, she woke up from her nap and glanced at her watch. It was nine o'clock and there was still no sign of Betina. Maxine called the shop and Betina answered the phone.

"Are you almost finished?"

"Almost, babe. Don't wait up for me. I'll be home soon."

"How soon?"

"Oh, I don't know. I'm getting some things together for our accountant. I have an appointment with the Tax Princess tomorrow."

"Then wake me up when you get home. It feels like forever since I've seen you."

"I will. Now go to bed, baby."

Maxine hung up the phone and threw some water on her face to wake herself up. She drove over to the shop and saw Betina's car in the parking lot. She knocked on the door and a surprised Betina peeked through the side drapes.

"What are you doing here?" she asked as she opened the door.

"I thought maybe I could help you with something and maybe get you home at a reasonable hour."

"Oh . . . well . . . uh . . . how thoughtful of you. Thanks." Betina waved her hand in the direction of the back of the shop. "Did you have dinner? There's some leftover pizza from lunch. Help yourself."

Every time Maxine entered Hair Today, she was reminded of the time she caught Betina giving one of her exes a haircut in that vibrating chair Joey had purchased several years ago. She and Betina had only been dating a short while, but they were serious about each other. Once they had gotten rid of the ex that night, the two of them had some of the greatest sex Maxine could ever remember.

"When did your last customer leave?" Maxine asked.

"A while ago."

She looked around the small back room that was used as an office. There was a box full of receipts, canceled checks, and bills on a card table. The cold pizza was on the counter. She helped herself to a slice and sat down at the table.

"I'm getting the feeling you're avoiding me," Maxine said, coming right to the point.

"What? Why would I do that?"

"You tell me."

"I've been busy."

"You've been busy before and never kept these kinds of hours."

"I'm in therapy now. That's thrown off my schedule."

"You've been getting home late and slipping into bed, making sure not to wake me up. Why is that?"

"I don't know what you're talking about," Betina said. "Besides, you need the rest. No one wants a sleepy surgeon."

Maxine heard the change in her voice before she saw the tears in her eyes.

"I know what you're doing," Maxine said quietly. "If you're worried about the sex—"

"Worried about it? What's there to worry about?"

Betina was crying now and finally stopped trying to hide it. Maxine wanted to hold her and reached for her hand, but Betina pulled away from her.

"You don't get it, Maxie," she said with a sniff.

Reeling from Betina's rejection, Maxine felt a sudden ache in her heart and a sense of panic in her stomach. With a hoarse voice laced with emotion, Maxine said, "What is it I'm not getting?"

"The one thing that's always made us so strong. The one thing that we've always shared and been able to depend on."

Maxine waited for her to finish the statement, but Betina seemed to withdraw and shut down right before her eyes—like a wind-up toy needing another turn of the key.

"What 'thing' is that?" Maxine whispered. "Tell me what you're thinking."

She waited for her to continue, but Betina had that blank stare and glassy look in her eyes again. Maxine was determined to get to the bottom of things no matter how painful it was for them. She wanted this resolved now.

"Betina."

She got no response from her, so Maxine reached over and touched her hand again. Betina blinked a few times and then slowly pulled her hand away.

"Tell me what you're thinking," Maxine said. "Please, baby. Talk to me."

After a moment, Betina said, "Dr. Miller."

"What about Dr. Miller?"

Betina looked away and picked up the pizza slice she had been nibbling on earlier. "She wants to keep me on those zombie pills for a year before trying something else."

Maxine took a deep breath. "Then that's what you need to do."

"And Laverne says I can't change shrinks. I have to stick with this Dr. Miller."

"I think that's good advice."

"I trust Laverne."

Maxine took another bite of pizza, but didn't have much of an appetite. She was still stunned from Betina's unwillingness to be touched.

"Let's go back to what you were saying earlier," Maxine said. "You mentioned something about the one thing that made us strong. What were you referring to?"

"I knew it," Betina said accusingly. "You don't get it, do you?"

197

"What do *you* think that one thing is?"

"It's sex, Maxie. Mind-boggling, toe-curling, wild sex. Hot sex on a carnival ride. Hot sex at the zoo. Hot sex in an elevator. *That's* the thing we've always shared and been able to depend on."

Maxine could feel the tears on their way and seconds later they rolled down her cheeks. She cleared her throat before speaking again.

"That might have been the way things were in the beginning," Maxine said quietly, "but that's not the way I see them now."

Betina dropped the rest of her pizza slice back into the box. "Now?" she said. "Now you have a lover who can't have sex."

"What?"

"Well, at least a lover who can't enjoy sex anymore and it'll be this way for a whole year if that Dr. Miller has her way."

"Then it sounds to me like you're saying if there's no more hot sex, then we've got nothing. Is that what I'm hearing?"

Betina closed the pizza box and stuffed it back in the refrigerator. She didn't answer, and Maxine felt physically ill.

Chapter Twenty-six

Maxine sat there with her in shocked silence. Neither seemed to know what to say. Finally, Maxine asked what else Betina had to do before she could leave for the evening.

Betina shrugged. "It's all in the box. That's more than the Tax Princess is used to getting from us."

"Then let's go home."

Betina slowly put her head in her hands and began to sob. The sound made Maxine's heart ache. She wanted to take Betina in her arms, but hesitated, fearing rejection again. *Fuck it*, she thought, and got up from the table and went to her.

"Don't cry, baby. Please."

"Oh, Maxie," she sobbed into Maxine's neck. "What's happening to me?"

"It's a lot of things all at once," Maxine whispered. At that moment she was just glad Betina didn't push her away again.

"Like what? What could it be? I'm doing everything I'm supposed to do. I'm going to therapy, I'm taking those zombie pills—"

"It could be a number of things in addition to the medication. Nothing will be an instant fix, not to mention you're probably PMSing. It's just going to take time."

Betina sniffed and nodded slowly.

Maxine held her at arm's length and looked into her eyes. "How could you think that sex would mean more to me than you do? More than our life together? Where did that come from?"

"You enjoy it so much. *We* enjoy it so much." She brushed away her tears with the back of her hand. "You could have anyone you wanted. You see all those women all day long . . . and you're smart . . . and funny . . . and sexy and . . . hell, you had that one patient tell you she felt like you two were in a long-term relationship because you'd seen her naked six times."

"What does all of that have to do with anything?"

Betina started to cry again. She reached for a Papa John's Pizza napkin on the card table and dabbed at her nose with it.

"I'm in love with you," Maxine said, her voice breaking as she spoke. "How could you doubt that or question it? Talk about *me* not getting it."

Betina sniffed again. "You still love me even though my clit's broke?"

Maxine hugged her and couldn't keep the chuckle inside any longer. "She's not broken, baby," she whispered as their foreheads touched. "Maybe she just needs a little break . . . or a rest . . . or a time-out."

"She's never needed a break before," Betina said with a sniff. "And she's been around for years, you know."

Maxine took her into her arms again. "Let's go home. We'll get in our bed and I'll hold you until you fall asleep."

Betina hugged her fiercely. "So you still love me? You won't leave me because of this?"

"Why would I leave you?" She returned the hug and didn't want to let go of her. "What have you been thinking? Where is this coming from all of a sudden?"

Betina sniffed. "You love all that wild sex as much as I do. If one of us isn't enjoying it anymore, that's like a major thing in our lives, Maxie. Our very foundation's been rattled. What else do we have? This is scarin' the hell out of me. Why would you want to stay with me now? What lesbian wants to stay with a lover with a broken clit?"

"Wow," Maxine said. "You're *really* not getting it! Sex isn't who we are and it's not all there is to Maxine and Betina. We have love. We have a home together. We have friends who care about us. We have each other. We have stickability, for crissakes! Or at least I *thought* we did! Sex is just a part of our lives. It's not the basis for our existence." She kissed her gently on the lips. "If we never have another night of wild sex together, my life will still be complete just knowing I have you in it. With or without a broken clit."

Let's hope the American Board of Obstetrics and Gynecology never knows I said such a thing, Maxine thought.

Betina threw her arms around Maxine's neck again. "Listen to you! Saying all the right things to me when I need to hear them!"

"So tell me something," Maxine said. "Suppose our roles were reversed. Suppose I was the one with the sexual problem." Maxine looked at her and had trouble forming the words she wanted to say next. She finally took a deep breath and asked, "Would you leave me because of that?"

They continued to look at each other for a moment and Maxine could almost see the wheels turning in Betina's head. Her hesitation was what Maxine had been dreading ever since this particular train of thought came into being. To Maxine, the answer was obvious. Even though they had never taken the "for better or for worse" or the "in sickness and in health" vows, that's the way she felt about Betina in her heart. Maxine loved her for who she was on the inside, not how many orgasms there would be in their future. Maxine was in this for the long haul and Betina's silence as the seconds ticked away was so loud and deafening that she was stunned by it. This was the first time Maxine had ever been faced with how differently they viewed their relationship. It was also the first time she felt as though she didn't really know the Betina Abbott who stood in front of her now.

Maxine picked up her car keys. The silence was unbearable. She wished dozens of times already that she had never uttered the question. Two minutes ago things were strained and confusing, but at least they were a loving, nurturing couple. Now Maxine was somewhere she'd never been before, and it was a place she didn't like.

"I guess I have my answer," she said.

Betina was silent and stared, speechless. She stood there as if in shock.

With tears blurring her vision, Maxine turned away. "I'm going home."

Walking in a daze, she left the shop and got in her car. Tears burned in her throat and Maxine thought she might get sick. Driving out of Hair Today's parking lot and through the late-night traffic, all she could think about was how different the two of them were.

How could she place such a high priority on sex in our relationship? Maxine wondered. *How long would she have stayed with me if the sexual problems had been mine instead of hers?*

Maxine blinked several times and swallowed to keep the bile from rising up into her throat. Weaving her way through traffic, she was home before she knew it. Arriving there alone made her stomach queasy again. Maxine got into the house and went directly to the bathroom and threw up.

The alarm woke her at five-thirty in the morning. Maxine had a slight headache and hoped to take care of it with some aspirin and strong coffee. Betina hadn't slept in their bed the night before, so Maxine went through the house looking for her. Betina's car wasn't in the garage either. *She must've stayed at the shop last night,* she thought. That made her sad and Maxine started to cry again. *You have to stop this,* she reminded herself. *You need to be in surgery in ninety minutes.*

Maxine took a hot shower and mentally reviewed her schedule for the day. She wouldn't be free to call Betina until later in the morning. Maxine had a hysterectomy and a cesarean scheduled for that morning. At least the aspirins were working by the time she got out of the shower.

Maxine took the stack of messages Mona handed to her and shuffled through them quickly. None were from Betina. Maxine went into her office and dialed the number for Hair Today. Joey answered the phone.

"Can I speak to Betina please?"

"What the hell's going on?" Joey whispered into the phone. "Her butt's draggin' today."

"Let me talk to her."

"She told me first thing this morning that she didn't want to talk to you yet in case you called."

"Fine."

"What's going on?"

"You ask her."

"She's not talkin'. I'm getting the silent treatment again. She's not even chatting-up the clients."

"Well, she knows how to reach me. I guess she'll do that when she's ready."

"Not even a hint about what's going on? This isn't like you two. You've always kept your fights and arguments at home."

"I'm sorry, Joey. I can't talk about this now. Tell her I called."

"Oh!" Joey said, then he laughed. "She just smacked a client on his bald head with a comb. He must've rubbed his arm across her boobs again."

Maxine smiled and knew exactly who the client was. Betina always had something to say when he'd been in to see her. At that moment, Maxine missed her so much she wanted to leave the office, drive over to the shop and just hold her.

"Tell her I called," she said and then hung up. Maxine knew that if she stayed on the phone with him any longer, she would cry.

She went home after work to an empty house. There was a note from Betina on the refrigerator stating that she had picked up some of her clothes and that she would be staying at the shop for a few days until her head was more clear. She also wrote that she would prefer that Maxine not be in touch with her for a while.

Just great, Maxine thought. She made a sandwich and decided to work on her paper until she got sleepy. Hopefully, going over her research would keep her mind too occupied to dwell on how her life was falling apart. After an hour or so of organizing her research, she decided to go to bed. The house was quiet, and as she made her way to the bedroom, everything reminded Maxine of Betina.

She slipped into bed and wondered what Betina was doing at that moment. The shop had a small area in the back with a shower. The restroom for customers was small, but nice and functional. Maxine wondered where Betina was sleeping and worried about whether or not she was taking her medication or eating properly.

Maxine knew she would sleep better if she heard some news about Betina, so she called Joey on his cell phone. The gay-boy music was just as loud as usual when she caught him at this hour.

"Joey," Maxine said. "How was Betina this afternoon?" She didn't want to tell him too much of their business. Maxine was still a little shocked that Betina had chosen not to come home yet.

"She cried off and on all day," he said, "but she's supposedly seeing her therapist once a day now, so I'm hoping that helps. Isn't she home yet? What time is it?"

"Not yet," Maxine said. "So she's still depressed."

"If anything, she's worse than before."

"Okay," Maxine said with a sigh. She didn't need to hear that before trying to sleep. "Thanks. I'll be in touch." She hung up the phone and set her alarm. Before Maxine could turn the light out, the phone rang. It was Elaine.

"Breakfast in the morning, Dr. Weston?"

Maxine smiled. "Sure. I don't have surgery, so I can make it. Same time. Same place."

They hung up and before Maxine could get comfortable under the covers, the phone rang again. This time it was Betina.

"Hi," she said with a sniff. "I miss you."

Just the sound of her voice made the tears start to flow. Maxine had done so well all evening.

"I miss you, too," Maxine said quietly. "Where are you?"

"At the shop. In one of those cheap lawn chairs. I bought a cot, then almost broke a nail getting it out of the box, so Laverne had a lawn chair to loan me."

"I'm glad you called."

"I needed to hear your voice. I miss you."

"Why don't you come home?" Maxine whispered. To speak any louder would have betrayed the sadness she felt. She didn't mind so much Betina hearing it; Maxine herself didn't like hearing it either.

"I can't. Not yet." Betina sniffed and then loudly blew her nose. "I'm working through some things with Laverne about my family. She's helping me come to terms with my anger. It's just all so messed up, Maxie."

Maxine was at a loss as to what to say. *When your lover is hurting,* she thought, *you want to do all you can to help them.* As much as she wanted Betina to feel better, Maxine also found herself resenting Laverne Simon for all the time she was able to spend with Betina. *She's learning about her deepest feelings, secrets, and emotions,* Maxine thought. *Get a grip. Laverne's there to help. Get over it already.*

"When can I see you?" Maxine asked.

"I don't know."

"You don't have to stay there at the shop. We have two other bedrooms here in the . . ." Maxine stopped. Her voice broke and she

205

couldn't finish the sentence. She heard Betina on the other end of the line blowing her nose. Maxine reached for a tissue and did the same thing.

"If I'm there in the house with you," Betina said in a husky voice full of emotion, "I'll want to be in our bed . . . with you."

"Why is that such a bad thing? We can be in the same bed and not have—"

"I'm dealing with two separate things now, Maxie. They're both about to crush me emotionally. I'm hanging on by a thread and I'm doing the best I can." Betina's voice got a little stronger as she continued. "Actually, I'm now having to deal with three things and it all keeps piling up on me. Not only that, I have to work through how the zombie pills keep taking all the fun out of my life just so I can get up every morning. It's not fair. Oh, and that's another thing. Laverne likes telling me how nowhere is it written that life has to be fair, so I guess I'm not in a very good place right now."

Maxine wasn't sure she liked Laverne at all any longer.

"Can I at least hear about the issues facing you?" Maxine asked. "And the progress you're making?"

"My relationship with my parents," Betina said. "I have all this anger inside. Laverne thinks all I might need from them is just an apology. Once they figured out who the porn magazines really belonged to, they didn't apologize to me. It has to be more complicated than that, but basically it's the bottom line with that issue."

Maxine shrugged. "That makes sense. What else? What other things are being addressed?"

Betina sighed. "I'm so mad at my clit, we're not speaking."

They shared a laugh together over that.

"Dr. Miller promised to wean me off the Zoloft and then try something else. I had to pitch a little fit to get her to agree to that, so there's another issue. Then," Betina said, "there's you."

Maxine heard her sniff again and there was some sort of hiccup that came out of her before Betina began to sob into the phone. Hearing it made Maxine's heart ache all over again.

Chapter Twenty-seven

Maxine let her cry into the phone for a while and even shed more tears of her own. Finally after that wave of emotion had passed, Maxine asked her to explain what she had meant by her "then there's you" comment.

"I'm still processing it, Maxie," Betina said with a sniff. "You threw me off balance with that question you asked me the other night . . . about how different things would be if you were the one with the sexual problems. It's made me stop and reevaluate so many things about myself. Like who I am and what I want from my life."

Maxine could feel her heart beginning to ache again. She gripped the phone and closed her eyes as the tears slowly rolled down her cheeks. *If she even had to think about it for a matter of seconds, then we've never been on the same page about our relationship,* Maxine realized. *For me our relationship became a close, loving partnership after only a few weeks, but apparently for her our time together was never more than a wild sex romp.*

Maxine leaned her head back and felt nauseous again. To think she had been living a lie these past five years made her wonder now what exactly had been taking place in her own life all this time.

"Anyway," Betina said, "that's what Laverne and I are working on now. She's trying to help me sort through a lot of things at once, but my relationship with you is a priority now."

Maxine didn't say anything. She couldn't say anything. She felt as though her life these past few years had been a sham. *Where have you been all this time?* she wondered. *How could you not know she cared more about sex than she cared about you?*

"Laverne's good at what she does," Betina said. "Already she knows me so well it surprises me sometimes." She sighed heavily, then whispered, "I miss you."

"Do you? Or do you just miss the sex?"

The gasp Maxine heard on the other end of the phone didn't make her feel any better, and neither did asking the question and getting it all out in the open again. She didn't want to spend another night crying herself to sleep.

"I can't do this on the phone," Betina said in a whisper.

"Let me know when you and Laverne come up with an answer for me, but right now I need to get some sleep."

Betina hung up without even saying good-bye.

Maxine was finally beginning to doze off when she heard a noise in the house. With her heart racing, she sat up in bed to listen and focus better. She saw a figure in the doorway, and then heard Betina's voice. "Maxie?"

"You scared the crap out of me."

"I'm sorry. I couldn't stop thinking about you. I'm a wreck."

"I'm not doing so well either. What time is it?" Maxine squinted in the direction of the clock.

"It's ten-thirty."

"Come to bed. I have to get up early for surgery in the morning."

"Just give me a few minutes. Please." Betina sat on the edge of the bed. "I can't go on another second knowing that you think all I'm interested in is having sex with you."

"Oh, yeah? It took you two days to figure that out?"

"Your question the other night made me think about things I'd never considered before," Betina said. "In all honesty, I *did* think the main thing we had going for us was the sex. That's why I freaked out so much when my clitoris stopped responding like it used to." She smoothed out the bedspread with the palm of her hand. "Laverne told me I had to stop saying that my clit was broke. I need to refer to her by her official name. And since clitorises aren't mechanical, they can't really break."

Bless you, Laverne, Maxine thought. She was finally beginning to wake up and tugged on the covers, pulling them up over her bare breasts against the air conditioned chill in the room.

"Anyway," Betina continued, "I've come to realize what our life together consists of. I can't believe the way I've been taking so many things for granted." She looked at Maxine with tear-swollen eyes. "And to think I had the nerve to razz you about not ever ordering a pizza." Betina looked away again. "When you asked about the possibility of our situations being reversed, I was more in shock than anything else. I knew that I loved you, but everything with us always seemed so wound up in sexual energy. We feed off each other so well. I can see you across a crowded room and feel the most wonderful sensations race through my body. No one else does that to me, and no one has ever made me feel the way you do."

Betina stopped and reached toward the nightstand. Maxine handed the tissue box to her.

"It's like I'm only half of something when I'm not with you," Betina said. "I'm a whole person and I even like the person that Betina is becoming these days, but there's another part of me that isn't complete without you."

Betina smoothed out more imaginary wrinkles in the bedspread as she talked. Maxine felt a huge sigh of relief as her heart began to swell with emotion.

"So it's not just the fabulous sex and the wild and lewd things we like to do together, Maxie. It's the mere essence and magic in what we are when we're together. I was so freaked out about losing my ability to have an orgasm that I let it overshadow the most important thing in my life." Betina blinked back tears, then after a moment she whispered, "Well, aren't you gonna ask me what the most important thing in my life is?"

Maxine smiled and felt a sense of warmth spread through her body. She slid her hand across the bed and touched Betina's fingers. "I know already."

Woody was due back the next day, so Maxine's breakneck pace at work would only last another twenty-four hours. She had coaxed Betina into staying with her the night before and they fell asleep in each other's arms. Betina told her that the reason she hadn't wanted to come home was because she had been afraid to tell Maxine that she didn't want to try making love again so soon.

"I need to get this zombie poison out of my system first," she said while snuggling into Maxine's arms. "Dr. Miller says the Welbutrin should work better for me. I just can't have another series of clitoris failures so soon, Maxie. Whoever thought I'd be afraid to have sex?"

"There's nothing to be afraid of, baby. If you don't have an orgasm, no one else has to know about it." She gave her an extra firm hug. "But we can wait as long as you think you need to."

"I keep thinking I'll give myself a heart attack stressing over it and trying to make it happen." Betina kissed Maxine's bare shoulder. "But just because my dewdrop is out of commission, that doesn't mean we can't give you the attention you deserve."

"I'll take you up on that when I'm more awake," Maxine said just before they both drifted off to sleep.

210

It was so good to have Betina home again that Maxine didn't want to leave the house the next morning, but she had promised to meet Elaine for breakfast. *We'll work things out,* she thought. *We'll take our time and work things out.*

After an early breakfast with Elaine, Maxine did some thinking on her way to the hospital. *Betina mentioned still having so much anger over what happened with her parents and Joey,* she thought. *Maybe a showdown with them would help clear the air.*

Maxine kept going back to that idea off and on all morning until finally she decided to call Joey.

"Do you have an address for your parents in Hawaii?" Maxine asked him a few hours later.

"Honolulu," Joey said.

"Can you be more specific? Small state—big city."

"I can probably get it from one of my aunts," Joey said. "Or maybe the phone book? Have you tried there?"

"This is important," Maxine said. "There might even be something in it for you if you help me out with this, big boy."

Mona knocked on her door again and poked her head inside Maxine's office. "Lunch is here and you've got one in the chute."

Maxine waved in her direction. She could hear Joey's laughter on the other end of the phone. She needed to make this quick. She had to see another patient and then eat her lunch on the way over to the hospital for a hysterectomy scheduled for that afternoon. To Joey she said, "Just see what you can find out for me please, and then leave a message with my receptionist."

Maxine got the address and phone number for Joseph and Penny Abbott in Honolulu, Hawaii. She placed a call to the Abbott residence after seeing her last patient for the day. Maxine was exhausted. *Thank the Goddess Woody's coming back tomorrow,* she thought.

211

"Aloha," the perky feminine voice said.

"Penny Abbott?"

"Yes. Who is this?"

"Dr. Maxine Weston from San Antonio, Texas."

There was dead silence. Being fully aware of the power her "doctor" title could have in certain situations, she was glad to have Penny Abbott's attention. It usually helped to get her a better table in a restaurant and it enabled her to have an excellent parking space at a hospital.

"Is it one of my children?" the woman asked quietly. "Has something happened to one of them?"

"I'm actually calling in reference to Betina," Maxine said.

"Oh, dear God. Is she hurt? Has she been in an accident?"

Maxine took her time and brought Mrs. Abbott down easily. "I'm Betina's partner," she said. When Maxine didn't hear Mrs. Abbott say anything, she added, "I'm her lover." Maxine went on to explain Betina's recent bouts with depression and her problems with anger and resentment related to the incident with her brother and the magazines.

"I see," Penny Abbott said. "So you're calling as her . . . uh . . . Betina's partner and not her doctor."

"Yes. That's correct. And as her partner, I think there are several things that have been ignored far too long."

"You know, Dr. Weston," Penny Abbott said, "I think that misunderstanding over those awful magazines is what made my daughter believe she might be a lesbian. The revulsion she must've felt during that time. She never denied they were hers. Once we learned the awful truth, there wasn't much we could do about what had happened."

"You could've apologized."

"What good would that have done? Besides, there were other things going on at the time."

"What other things?"

"My husband's older brother was gay. He had been estranged from the family for years."

"Betina never mentioned having a gay uncle."

"The twins never knew him. He lived in Seattle and died of AIDS. About the time the twins were teenagers, there were reports of a genetic link for homosexuals. Because of my husband's brother . . . well . . . when the twins announced they were gay, it was extremely hard on us. Especially my husband."

"So Betina and Joey never knew they had a gay uncle?"

"They knew they had an uncle, but they didn't know he was gay."

"Sounds to me like you and your husband needed therapy more than your kids did."

There was silence for a moment, then Penny said, "That's probably more true than you know."

"Well, right now Betina needs some closure. The incident with the magazines has come back to haunt her. I would like to see that resolved."

Penny Abbott assured her that she and her husband wanted to see their daughter again. By the time they were into the next ten minutes of the conversation, Maxine had the woman right where she wanted her.

Maxine drove over to Hair Today after work and saw Betina's car in the parking lot and Joey coming out of the shop on his way home for the day.

"Is Betina still working?"

"She's finishing up her last client," he said. "It was a slow day."

"I want to talk to both of you. Can you have dinner with us? I'm buying."

"You said the magic words."

They went back inside and found Betina combing and blow drying a young woman's hair. Maxine and Joey went in the back to

213

the break area. She saw a stack of supply catalogs on a counter and wondered how long Betina's depression would have festered had the misrouted porn magazine not been discovered. *Fate was in the hands of the Goddess,* she thought.

"What's the occasion?" Joey asked. He picked up a stack of catalogs and thumbed through the one on top.

"I spoke with your mother today."

Joey sat up and dropped the catalog on the floor. His blue eyes were wide with surprise. "You did?"

"What are the chances of you two being able to close the shop for a few days?"

"None. We need the money and we have standing appointments every week."

"Not even for a free trip to Hawaii?"

Joey's eyes grew even wider and registered that same surprised expression again. "Did you say *free* trip to Hawaii?"

"Free. You and Betina."

"You wouldn't be going with us?"

"I can't get away right now."

"Free," he said, and picked up the catalog that had fallen on the floor. "You'll pay for everything?"

Maxine nodded.

"What's the catch?"

"So you'll close the shop?"

"Hell yes we'll close the shop! This is Hawaii! *Free* Hawaii. Now tell me what the catch is."

"All I want you to do while you're there is make sure you and Betina spend time with your parents, and that the three of you apologize to her for the magazine incident."

"What makes you think my parents will see us? They don't like me or my lifestyle."

"How your parents relate to you isn't the priority at the moment," Maxine said, "but I think it's a good idea that the four of you make the most of this opportunity. A free trip to Hawaii probably won't come along again anytime soon."

"No shit."

"So will you do it? Can the shop be closed for a few days?"

"How long are you willing to support this endeavor?" Joey asked. "It might take a few days to get them to agree to an apology."

"I'm willing to pay for a week's worth of expenses for the both of you."

"Nice hotel on the beach?"

"Are there any other kind in Hawaii? Seven days and three apologies," Maxine said. "I'll pay your airfare and expenses for seven days, while you make sure Betina gets her apologies."

"First class airline tickets?"

"No!" Maxine said with a laugh.

"Then how about some spending money while I'm there?"

"What a nice surprise," Betina said after the client left. She kissed Maxine lightly on the lips.

"Pick a place for dinner," Maxine said. "I have something to discuss with both of you."

They convoyed to a coffee shop down the street and were seated right away.

Maxine explained about talking to Penny Abbott earlier in the day.

"You actually talked to my mother?" Betina said.

"Yes, I did. We had a pleasant conversation."

"How did you find her?"

Maxine shrugged. "I knew your parents were in Hawaii. It's not that big of a place." She noticed Joey trying his best to appear nonchalant by studying a flyer on the various dinner specials.

"Why would you call her?" Betina asked, snatching up a menu.

Maxine took a deep breath and calmly said, "I'm getting to that. It seems as though your parents want to see you."

"My mother said that?" Betina asked, barely able to control her gasp of surprise.

"She did," Maxine confirmed.

"Well . . . hmm . . ."

"So I'm proposing that both of you go to Hawaii and see your parents," Maxine said.

"Both of us?" Betina said. "Just me and Joey? You won't be going with us?"

"I can't get away right now. Woody's just getting back from vacation and I have clinic obligations with Blanche I can't get out of."

Betina looked at her suspiciously and then glanced at her brother. Shaking her blond head, Betina said, "We can't close the shop. We've got regular appointments."

"We can make some arrangements," Joey said. "I'll make all the calls."

Betina looked closely at her brother then shook her head again.

"Free Hawaii," he reminded her. "Think about it, Betina. Free Hawaii."

After a moment, Betina said, "Well, when would we have to go?"

"As soon as you two can arrange to close the shop for a few days," Maxine said. It was the first time since this whole conversation began that Maxine felt hopeful about her offer. She hadn't anticipated Betina's reluctance.

"Your mother expressed an interest in seeing you," Maxine said. "I thought it would be good if Joey went along with you."

"Him?" Betina said, pointing a fork in Joey's direction. "He'll be laying out on the beach all day or sipping those foo-foo umbrella drinks by the pool! What good will he be?"

"She's given me a mission," Joey said indignantly in his own defense.

"Why does my mother want to see us now? After all this time?"

"You can ask her that when you see her," Maxine said. *And by then you'll be there already and hopefully have your three apologies before we see each other again*, she thought.

216

Betina shook her head. "I don't know. What kind of vacation is this? I'm taking my brother along instead of my lover. I see him too much as it is already. Ten hours a day side-by-side snipping hair and covering up roots. I need a vacation *away* from him."

"It's *Hawaii*," Joey said, "and it's *free*."

Betina looked at Maxine across the table. "What am I gonna do there without you?"

"Spend some quality time with your parents," Maxine said softly.

"You'll only have to see me once," Joey assured her. "I promise. Just once."

"Gay bars and nude beaches," Betina said. "I already *know* where you'll be."

Chapter Twenty-eight

Once Maxine got a firm date from Joey on when the shop would be closed, she had Mona and her office crew search for the best travel package for Hawaii. Maxine was relieved when Betina finally began to get excited about the trip and stopped worrying so much about seeing her parents again. What really got Betina's attention was realizing she needed new clothes to wear there. Maxine happily opened her wallet and came home in the evenings to a lover who couldn't wait to show off her purchases for the day.

"Oh, baby, this is such a wonderful idea," Betina said. She sat down on the sofa and piled the shopping bags all around them. "I'm feeling a lot better on this new medication."

Maxine pulled a peach-colored silk blouse from a bag.

"But I'm still mad at my clitoris," Betina admitted. "We're not on speaking terms yet."

"Well, the minute your clitoris begins to say something, make sure you give me a call. I can't be missing any of that."

"Oh! Look at this!" Betina said as she unfolded another blouse.

Maxine loved hearing the joy and delight in Betina's voice. *Yes,* Maxine thought. *She's sounding like her old self a little more each day.*

"I wish you were going with us," Betina said with a pout.

Maxine laughed. "Someone has to stay here and pay for all of this, you know."

Joey made an elaborate sign to put on the door of the shop that said: Gone Fishing—In Hawaii!

"Fishing?" Maxine said when she heard about the sign. "Have either of you ever *been* fishing?"

"We saw a video on it once," Betina said. "Joey thought it would make us sound more butch."

Maxine made arrangements to take them to the airport the morning they were to leave.

"Seven days, babe," Maxine said while loading up the last of Betina's four huge suitcases in the car. "You've got enough stuff here to last you for a month."

"And it's all essential."

"How many of these bags are full of shoes?"

"All essential," Betina said again.

"I hope we have room for Joey's stuff in my car."

"How much room can a thong and sunscreen take up?" Betina asked.

Maxine chuckled and opened the car door for her. They had to pick up Joey and still miss most of the morning traffic on the way to the airport. When they got to Joey's house, he was ready and out the front door in a hurry. A sleepy young man in a loose bathrobe waved from the doorway.

"Who's that?" Betina asked him.

"The dog sitter," Joey said.

"I'm glad I didn't volunteer for that job," Maxine said.

"Why, baby?" Betina asked. "You'd look cute in nothing but a bathrobe."

Joey had two suitcases that barely fit in Maxine's backseat.

"Will you look at that?" Betina said, pointing to his luggage. "One suitcase for the thong and sunscreen and another one for all his mousse."

"Shuddup!" Joey said with a laugh and a thump on his sister's arm.

"Everyone have their IDs and itineraries?" Maxine asked.

"Oh!" Joey said. He patted himself down and finally came up with his wallet. "Got it. I'm ready."

The three of them waved at the sleepy dog sitter and were on their way.

"Do you even know his name?" Betina asked her brother.

"What kind of question is that?" came Joey's indignant reply.

"Yeah, really," Maxine agreed.

"Well, do you?" Betina insisted.

"Of course I do! It's Eddie. Eddie something or other."

Maxine got them to the airport a little later than she would have liked, but they had enough time for hugs at the curb. Betina found a Sky Cap to help them with their luggage and while she fussed with that, Maxine slipped Joey five hundred dollars for spending money as promised.

"Thanks," he said when he hugged her.

"Bring her back to me with three sincere apologies," Maxine said. "I don't care what you do the rest of the time you're there. Oh, and it's best if she not drink with the medication she's taking."

"I know. She knows it, too. She'll be fine. I promise. I want her to get better, too, you know."

Betina came around the back of the car with her arms open. "I'm going to miss you," she said, putting her arms around her and holding Maxine tightly. "I wish you were going with me."

"I do, too. Maybe we can get away together later in the summer."

"I'll call you every night. My girls and I miss you already." She kissed Maxine on the lips and then hugged her again. Betina turned around and called out to the Sky Cap, "Don't get our bags mixed up. I don't want that thong-holder-thing anywhere near my luggage."

Once word got out that Maxine would be alone for a few days, the dinner invitations with friends started to come in. It was common knowledge what Maxine's idea of cooking meant. If she had to open three things, then she considered it cooking. A bag of chips, a container of dip, and a Diet Coke was considered cooking.

Blanche and Phoebe invited her over one night and then Cheryl and Elaine had her over for dinner the next. It was good to see her friends, but she missed Betina. When Maxine got home every evening, the house seemed so empty without her. Betina made sure there was a nice long message from Hawaii waiting for her in addition to the call Maxine would receive later in the evening. They stayed connected that way and caught each other up on how their days had gone. Betina was also sensitive to the time difference between Texas and Hawaii, and placed her calls around Maxine's sleep and work schedule.

"It's beautiful here, baby," Betina said. "It makes me miss you even more."

Maxine got comfortable in bed and knew she would sleep well after hearing Betina's voice.

"What did you do today?" Maxine asked her.

"Tourist things. The hotel had something set up. Joey's met someone already, so he's out of my hair. He made the arrangements for us to have dinner with Mom and Dad this evening. You know what that little shit wants me to do?" Betina said with a laugh. "He wants me to put something in my dress so it looks like I'm nine months pregnant when they first see me."

Maxine arched her brows. "I suggest you not take his advice."

"Well . . . *duh!* He just wants to make himself look better when they see us again. We had a good laugh over it, but I'm not doing it."

"Whew," Maxine said. She had a vision of a vast amount of money swirling down a drain. "Thank you."

"I'm nervous about seeing them."

"It'll be okay," Maxine said. "And if it's not, then fuck 'em."

Betina's laughter sounded delightful. "I'll let you know tomorrow how it went. Now go to sleep, baby. You have to get up early."

Several hours later Maxine heard the telephone ring and fumbled for it on the nightstand.

"Dr. Weston," she mumbled.

"Maxie," Betina said with giddy excitement in her voice. "I know you're asleep and I'm sorry for calling you so late, but I have to tell you what happened at dinner tonight! My parents apologized to me! You should've seen us. My mother started to cry, then my father got all choked up. Joey apologized first and then the other two chimed in! After that, the waterworks were on for sure. We were four crying Abbotts in a public restaurant. They all hugged me, and we laughed and started talking about things that happened when Joey and I were little. Oh, Maxie. It was a wonderful evening and I love you for making it possible."

Maxine smiled and felt a huge sense of relief.

"Baby," Betina whispered. "Thank you for loving me."

"You're welcome," Maxine said sleepily.

"Now hang up the phone. We'll talk more tomorrow."

Maxine took the phone away from her ear and pushed a few buttons in her sleep until the dial tone went away. The next morning when her alarm clock went off, she found the telephone still in bed with her.

"My mother and I had breakfast together today," Betina said, catching Maxine at the hospital having a late lunch with Elaine.

"So things are going well?" Maxine asked.

222

"*Very* well. Joey and my dad are playing golf. Can you imagine? It's cutting into Joey's thong-time on the beach, but he'll make up for that later this afternoon. We're having dinner with them again tonight. Oh, Maxie. I'm so happy! I can't believe how much better I feel!"

"Good." *Some of that might have to do with the new medication,* she thought while paying the cashier for her lunch and keeping the phone tucked against her ear.

"I miss you," Betina said.

"I miss you, too."

"I'll call you tonight."

Maxine closed her phone and slipped it into her lab coat pocket.

"When is she due back?" Elaine asked. She snagged a semi-clean table for them in the corner of the cafeteria.

"Tomorrow afternoon," Maxine said. "It's been a long seven days."

"Have dinner with us again tonight," Elaine said. "We both enjoy seeing you."

Maxine nodded. "Okay. Thanks."

The following afternoon, Maxine was paged for a delivery for one of Woody's patients. He was stuck in surgery and Maxine was on call. She had to make arrangements for someone else to pick up Joey and Betina from the airport. Phoebe was the only one reachable and with the day off. She didn't mind doing it at all, which was a big relief for Maxine.

"Thanks!" Maxine said into her cell phone. "I owe you."

It was a long, difficult delivery, and Maxine was exhausted by the time she arrived home that evening. But even though she was tired, it was wonderful walking into the house knowing she would find Betina asleep in their bed. Maxine felt as though things were right again and everything was in its proper place. As she neared the bedroom, Maxine could smell a mixture of Betina's perfume and the soap she used for her shower. The warmth Maxine felt was familiar

223

and welcomed. All Maxine knew was that when she was away from Betina for any length of time, she felt incomplete and out of focus. But now as she slowly undressed and took in the familiar sight of her sleeping lover in the bed, Maxine's heart was at peace again.

She slipped into bed and Betina turned over and met her halfway.

"Hold me," Betina said sleepily.

Maxine took her into her arms and couldn't believe how much she had missed her.

"A boy or a girl?" Betina mumbled.

"A boy."

Betina kissed the side of Maxine's face.

"Who loves you?" Maxine whispered.

"You do."

They both fell soundly asleep.

Maxine was able to talk to Betina only once in between patients the next day. Betina and Joey were busy at the nursing home getting as many of the residents as possible ready for the Blue Hair Night dance. Maxine finally caught up with her during a sneaker break that afternoon.

"Did you have lunch yet?" Betina asked.

"Not yet, but a drug rep's supposed to be by with something good soon. How about you?"

"Joey found us some peanut butter and jelly sandwiches. We had that in between haircuts and sets. No time for a real meal in the cafeteria. We've got a senior assembly line in progress here, so I need to go and get back to them."

"Do we still have a date for the dance?" Maxine asked. She was tired already and hoping they'd at least be able to leave the dance early.

"We're on," Betina said. "I'll meet you here in case you get held up. Oh, and bring more business cards! Might as well do a little pimping while we're at it."

Maxine's afternoon flew by until she saw her last patient. "My goodness," she said when she examined her. "How long have you been bleeding like this?"

"Since last night."

Maxine looked at her nurse. "Let's get her over to the hospital." To the patient she said, "Is someone here with you?"

"My husband's out there in the waiting room."

Maxine let her staff take care of all the arrangements while she went over to the hospital to check on the patient who had delivered the night before and another patient who had a hysterectomy the previous day. She would release them both tomorrow.

The surgery went well and Maxine was able to get something to eat in the hospital cafeteria before it closed up for the evening. After the surgery, she took a shower and changed in the hospital staff locker room. By the time Maxine reached the parking lot it was nearly midnight. She called Betina at home and didn't get an answer so she drove over to the nursing home and saw that both Betina and Joey's cars were still there. She could hear Fifties music as soon as she got out of her car.

Maxine went inside and noticed a few older residents in the main hallway. She opened the metal doors to the cafeteria and found the Blue Hair Night dance in full swing. She stood by the refreshment table and ladled punch into cups and set them on a tray. Across the room, Maxine saw Betina dancing with an older man in a wheelchair. When the song was over, the DJ made an announcement for the evening's last song just before "Sixteen Candles" began to play.

Betina waved to her from across the room and came over to the refreshment table.

"Dr. Weston," Betina said. "What a wonderful surprise. Can I have this dance?"

Maxine filled another cup with punch and set the ladle back into the punch bowl. Betina held out her hand and led her around the table and onto the dance floor. Once Betina was in her arms, Maxine felt the heat radiating from their bodies.

"I'm so glad you came," Betina said. "It seems like forever since I've seen you." She playfully moved her hand down Maxine's back and gently caressed her butt. "I have a surprise for you later."

"Really?" Maxine said. "What is it? I love surprises."

Betina leaned closer and brushed her lips against Maxine's ear. "I tried a little experiment this morning and I seem to be fully functional again."

Maxine leaned her head back and laughed. *Oh, how I love this woman*, she thought.

Betina nuzzled her nose against Maxine's ear. "So where would you like to try it tonight? The parking lot here at Shady Rest, or whatever this place is called? Or perhaps stall number three in the men's bathroom? Or maybe just take it home and howl at the moon?"

"Hmm," Maxine said, offering her a pensive look. "It's been a while since we've howled at the moon."

"I was just thinking that, too."

"But then again," Maxine whispered as her lips grazed Betina's ear, "how big do you think stall number three is anyway?"